HOPE FOR FAMILY

HOPE RANCH BOOK 5

ELIZABETH MADDREY

Cover design by Lynnette Bonner @ Indie Cover Designs

Published in the United States of America by Elizabeth Maddrey.
www.ElizabethMaddrey.com

1

Jade Clarke took a deep breath of the sharp, winter air and shoved her hands deeper into the pockets of her coat. The thick layer of snow glinted in the morning sun and hushed the everyday noises of the ranch. There were a few trails of footprints leading from the cabins toward the stable and main house, but otherwise the snow's surface was unbroken. Pristine.

"Morning, Jade." Tommy Russell, one of the workers at Hope Ranch, lifted his hand as he stepped out onto the porch of his cabin. "Nothing like starting the new year with snow."

The new year had officially started three days ago, but she understood his meaning. She blew out a breath and smiled as the air froze into a white cloud that drifted off in the light breeze. "I guess. It's never been an issue before."

"Guess not. This isn't California."

"No. It really isn't."

"You miss it?"

Did she? She shook her head. The big PR firm in L.A. felt like someone else's life—or maybe hers, but a lifetime ago. She'd only been at Hope Ranch since April. What was that, nine months? But it could be ten times that and it wouldn't feel any closer. "Not really. Maybe the beach."

He grinned. "I could use a week at the beach. But not in L.A. Mexico, maybe. Or some island in the Caribbean."

"Oh, yeah. Turquoise water and white sand? Sign me up." For the briefest moment, she got a flash of herself stretched out on a towel in her bathing suit beside a very nice pair of male legs. Whose legs? Didn't matter—she'd been without a man in her life for too long. Although her newfound faith in Jesus meant she couldn't just grab someone and go. Didn't it? She sighed. "I probably have to get a little more business before I can take that vacation, though."

Tommy nodded. "I'm not rushing off today, either. I'm sure Mel would have several choice words to say about that. Speaking of..."

Jade's eyebrows lifted. "What'd she do now?"

"Olivia. She's supposed to come down tomorrow for the rest of the week—it's her last week of winter break. Would you be willing to help Betsy entertain her if I'm doing an outside job? Mel grudgingly said Livy could watch while I worked if it was indoors, but she's worried Livy will catch cold if I'm fixing fences or something."

"That makes no sense."

"Mel isn't known for her logic. At this point, I think she make rules just to see if she can get me to argue with her. Then she'll have a reason to get huffy and not send her." He shrugged. "I'm trying to work on not playing into her hands. Would you mind? I know you're working, too, but I just want to have plans in place. She's going to ask."

Jade laughed. "Sure. I like kids. We'll go bug Indigo and learn how to spin or something. Or maybe we can go cross-country skiing. Wayne offered to teach me, and I think I'd like that."

"The meadow's great for that. I'll check on the equipment sizes. If we don't have stuff that'll work, I can grab something in Albuquerque when I drive down to pick her up."

"And neither of us will mention that skiing is outside where she might catch a chill, right?"

He pointed at her, his lips curving. "Exactly. But if—no, when—Mel asks her if she worked with her dad outside, she'll be able to say no. She hasn't forbidden Livy from being outside. Just working with me. I think it was her hope that would mean I'd say no to having her come."

"Sorry."

"Yeah, well. Sometimes the consequences of a bad decision last a long, long time." He shook his head and started down his cabin's steps. "Thanks, Jade. See ya at lunch?"

"Yeah. There's a rumor going around that it's chicken and dumplings."

"Yum." He grinned before flicking his fingers up in a brief wave and stomping through the snow toward the stable.

Jade watched him walk away. Maybe she wasn't supposed to be ogling guys, as a believer now, but if she called it appreciating the beauty of God's creation, maybe she could get away with it. It wasn't as if she was fantasizing about him. He just had a really great physique. Even bundled up for the cold.

She sighed and went back inside.

"You want some coffee, hon?" Elise looked over from where she filled her own mug in the kitchen.

"I can get it." It was still strange—even nine months later—to be living with the mother of her half-siblings. Jade's mother had painted Elise in such a horrible light that Jade had expected her to have fangs and claws. Jade should have known better. Her mother had been angry and bitter about everything. And she'd taken great joy, for lack of a better word, in spreading that darkness wherever she could.

"Nonsense. Sit down and warm back up. Did I hear you talking to Tommy?" Elise reached for another mug and poured in coffee.

"Yeah. I guess he's getting a late start. Or maybe he'd been back to the cabin for something." She reached for the mug as Elise came to the table and sat. "The snow's pretty."

"And cold." Elise smiled over the top of her coffee before sipping.

"And cold. It's true." Jade curled her hands around the mug, more interested right now in the heat than the liquid inside. "I mentioned the beach, and now I can't get the idea out of my head."

"You should go."

As if it were that easy. "Nah. I'm not quite there yet. But I will absolutely be earmarking part of my savings account for the Caribbean now. Maybe next winter. I have a video call with a prospective client at ten—if I can land her, and if I do a good job in her eyes, it's a whole new avenue of potential business."

"Oh?" Elise sipped.

Jade didn't have to answer. Elise was easy that way—content with whatever people were willing to give. Was it that part of Elise's personality that had allowed her to stay with Martin—Jade's father, and the father of Elise's kids—despite his serial straying? It was easy to talk to Elise, though. So Jade lined up her thoughts as she sipped her drink. "This woman is an indie author—she publishes her books herself. It's a big thing now, I'm learning. Anyway, there are a *ton* of people out there writing books and putting them for sale, and they do all their own social media and website stuff. So there's a new need for virtual assistants. So we'll see. I have some of the skill set she mentioned. It might not end up being a great fit, but then again it might."

"Well, that sounds kind of fun. And you pick things up so fast—I'm sure you could learn anything she needed you to do."

That had been Jade's thought, as well. It depended on what that entailed. But she was willing to give it a shot. There had to be a way to make enough money that she could talk the Hewitts into letting her pay rent. Or contribute to groceries. Or something that would mean she was earning her keep here. "I guess we'll see. Either way, I'll still have time to help Tommy out with his daughter if he needs."

"Do you actually think she'll come?" Elise shook her head. "I guess I don't."

"He's prepping like she is, so I guess he's pretty confident?" Wasn't he? It didn't matter, honestly. She could watch kids or not. "I guess we'll find out. This woman—his ex—she's really that bad?"

"From what Betsy has said, yes. And Betsy isn't one to speak ill."

No. She wasn't. "Huh. Then I hope for Tommy's sake his daughter gets to come. You can tell he misses her."

Elise nodded. "He's trying his hardest. I—I want you to know I'm sorry that Martin didn't do better by you."

"It's not your fault." Jade crossed her arms. She and Elise had tiptoed around the subject of her father for close to a year.

"It kind of is. We had an arrangement. I'm not proud of it. He broke it. But then he lied. I'm not stupid. I knew it was likely he had other kids—but I ignored the possibility and I probably pushed him into not being a father to you. I'm sorry for my part in that. I hope you can forgive me."

Jade reached over and touched Elise's hand. "I do. My mom—I loved her, you know? She was all I had. But she wasn't an easy person. I don't think she would have let Martin compromise. It was always all or nothing with her. In everything. He made the right choice with a clean break. I don't like it. But I can't blame him—or you—for it. Not anymore."

Elise's eyes filled and she looked away.

Jade stared down into her coffee. The words she'd just said hadn't been conscious thoughts, but the idea of them had been floating around in her brain for a while now—intensifying since she'd finally surrendered her heart to Jesus. A smile tugged at her lips—wasn't that a hilarious thing? Her mother had been so completely opposed to any organized religion. If someone had asked Jade how likely it was she'd ever be willing to attend church, she would have said zero.

Now she was up onstage with the worship band on Sundays when they needed a substitute.

Jade cleared her throat. "I'm going to get to work. I'll see you at lunch?"

Elise nodded but didn't speak.

Jade stood and patted the woman's shoulder lightly as she carried her coffee with her into her bedroom. She'd set up a desk in there, so it was a one-stop shop. Sometimes she'd venture into the living room with her laptop when she was sure Elise had gone on to help Indigo in the fiber cottage—or whatever else she got up to during the day.

They had a settled, quiet peace as roommates.

Jade didn't want to rock the boat.

Maybe that was less of an issue now.

"So? What did you think?" Wayne bent over to pick up his cross-country skis and turned to grin at Jade.

"I think tomorrow I'm going to hurt in muscles I didn't know I had." She laughed. "But it was fun. I need more practice. Obviously. You said it was like walking, but with skis on."

Wayne reached around to scratch his neck. "Well, now, I couldn't quite figure out how else to put it."

"I'll try to come up with a better description for you." She looked down at her skis and groaned. "I'm not sure I can still bend."

Wayne chuckled. "Sure you can. And I know for a fact that Maria said she'd make us her hot chocolate when we got back. Does that get you moving?"

Jade's mouth watered. "It does. She has a way."

With eyes full of mirth, Wayne took her skis and poles. "I'll store these. You go on in and let Maria know not to spare the whipped cream."

"All right. Thanks, Wayne."

He paused and waited until she met his eyes. "We're your grandparents too, you know."

She blinked and a lump formed in her throat. She nodded once and turned toward the mudroom door. No one at Hope Ranch pushed. But they were still there, quietly whittling away at her defenses. Did he want her to call him Grandpa?

Jade stomped the snow off and left the boots—although they were more like running shoes than the type of thing she associated with the word "boot"—just inside the door. She unwound her scarf and stuffed it in her hat before tucking the lot into her coat pocket. She shrugged off the coat, then hooked it on a peg and padded into the kitchen.

"You're back. Did you have fun?" Maria stirred a pot at the stove.

Jade sniffed. "Is that enchilada sauce?"

"Good nose. I'll start the chocolate now. Go and sit. You liked it?"

"I did. It's different than downhill."

"So different." Maria laughed and tapped the spoon on the side of the pot before setting it aside. She adjusted the heat on the burner and moved to the refrigerator. "We have good downhill skiing not far from here."

Jade slid onto one of the stools at the long counter that

formed one edge of the kitchen and separated the space from the family room. "Sure. Angel Fire, right? And Sandia isn't far, either."

"Mmmhmm. Or Pajarito Mountain, if you want someplace a little closer with a more local feel. Point being, there are some good options."

"It's not really my thing. I'm more likely to surf than ski." She got that flash of the white sand and teal water again as longing oozed into her heart. She was going to have to take a good, hard look at her bank account and see what it was going to take to make that beach vacation happen. "But cross-country skiing is something I can see myself doing."

"Next time you want to go, let me know. It's a good workout and the baby weight isn't coming off as easily this time as it did with Calvin." Maria turned the fire on under a new pot and stirred in milk.

Jade frowned. "You look amazing."

"Oh. Well. Thank you." Maria brushed a hand over her shirt. "It's reflex, you know?"

She nodded, even though she didn't really. One good thing about her mom was the sense of self-confidence—and maybe it bordered on arrogance—that she'd instilled. Jade hadn't struggled with low self-esteem. Too high? Yeah, that could be an issue.

"She's right." Wayne winked as he crossed through the kitchen and took the stool next to Jade. "All of the ladies of Hope Ranch are gorgeous just the way God made them. That said, we'd love to have you ski with us. You say the word and we'll set it up."

Maria laughed. "All right. I will. And in anticipation of that, I'll even join you for hot chocolate. I was going to beg off, but, well, life's short."

"That's the spirit." Wayne tugged his phone out of his shirt pocket and frowned at it.

"Something wrong?" Jade glanced over but didn't see anything other than the time on his screen.

"No. Probably not. Tommy said he'd let me know when his daughter's plane landed and I thought he said two for that."

"Isn't it close to four?" Jade craned her neck, trying to see into the kitchen to check the time on the stove clock.

"About. I'm sure it's fine. He probably got caught up with baggage claim and then a snack—or a need to run around before getting in the truck for the ride back here." Wayne slipped his phone back into his shirt pocket and gave it an absentminded pat. "Probably don't need to hold dinner for them, Maria."

Maria nodded. "All right. We'll still be on for five thirty. You're coming tonight, Jade, right?"

She hadn't planned to. The Hewitts had made it clear she was welcome to eat with them at any and every meal she chose. It was an invitation they made to anyone who lived and worked on the ranch. She usually only hung around for lunch. But between Maria's enchiladas and wanting to have a reason to hang out and see Tommy's kid? "Yeah. I think I will. Thanks."

2

Tommy wanted to punch something.

He'd waited at the door that all passengers had to use to leave the secured area of the airport until the foot traffic stopped. No teenager had walked alongside a smiling flight attendant. No one rushed those last couple steps to throw her arms around him.

Instead, it was the quizzical—and somewhat suspicious—look of a security guard. "Help you, sir?"

"Maybe? My daughter was supposed to be on the flight that just landed—is there a way to find out where she is?"

The security guard sprang into action, talking into his shoulder mic. At least they took the potential loss of a child seriously.

"Sir? Could you go to the check-in desk, please?"

Tommy looked back down the empty hallway and sighed. His daughter wasn't lost. Mel just hadn't put her on the plane. He'd bet everything he owned on it. But for now, all that was left was to follow the steps and be sure. "Yeah. Thanks."

The guard nodded and pointed in the right direction.

The airport wasn't huge, so it took very little time for Tommy to make his way to the correct place. He found a short line and waited for the two people in front of him to get checked in and on their way to wherever.

"Next, please."

He forced his lips to curve as he approached the woman at the desk. It wouldn't do anyone any good to start off combative. And it wasn't going to be the airline's fault anyway. This stank of Mel and her power plays. Tommy cleared his throat. "Is it possible to see if someone was on the plane that just landed? My daughter was supposed to be traveling to see me for the week . . ."

The woman's eyebrows lifted. "I'm not sure. Let me go find my manager."

"Thanks." He tucked his hands in his pockets. Should he call Mel? No. That was a terrible idea right now. He wasn't going to be able to be polite and, knowing her, she'd find some way to twist it and use it against him in court. Because they were very obviously headed back there. Maybe he should call his lawyer. Well, obviously he *should* call his lawyer, but maybe it was better to have confirmation first.

"Sir?" It was a man now. The woman from before hovered at his elbow. "I'm very sorry. We can't give out passenger information."

"Of course. Except this is my daughter, a minor, who was supposed to be flying unaccompanied." Tommy pulled out his phone and swiped to the confirmation email from when Mel had booked the tickets. He laid it on the desk and pushed it toward the man. "Her mother was supposed to put her on the plane this morning and I was to collect her. She never came off the plane. And since I didn't book the ticket, I can't log in to check anything. I just want to know where my kid is."

"Yes, sir. May I?" He gestured to the phone.

"Yeah, sure. Go for it." Tommy's blood boiled and it was all he could do to keep from spewing all over the airline employees. But it wasn't their fault. Maybe if he kept saying it, he'd remember it. They were doing their job. He shifted and stared at the empty chairs pushed against the wall. Where was Olivia?

"I'm sorry, sir, it seems this reservation was cancelled this morning by the purchaser." He pushed the phone across the desk with a sympathetic smile. "Perhaps she was unable to get in touch to let you know."

Tommy snorted as he reached for his phone. He offered a tight smile and a sharp nod. "Sorry to waste your time."

"Have a good day, sir."

Tommy shook his head. A good day wasn't even in the realm of possibility right now. He stormed through the airport, into the parking garage, and over to where he'd parked his truck. He kicked the tire before unlocking the door, climbing in, and banging his head on the steering wheel. Now what?

He sighed.

Tommy unlocked his phone and scrolled to his lawyer's contact and hit the phone icon before he could talk himself out of it. He wanted to call Mel and ask what the heck. He needed to talk to Don.

"This is Donald."

"Hey, Don. It's Tommy."

"Russell." Don dragged it out like they were greeting each other on the football field. "How's it going?"

Tommy had to smile. Everyone said not to make friends with your lawyer, but Don made that impossible. He still gave off the frat-boy surfer vibe, but when it came to court, that disappeared like a switch got flipped. Then he was a force to be reckoned with. It made Tommy glad to have him in his corner. "Well, do you hear a kid laughing in my truck right now?"

"That's today?" Tommy could picture Don straightening at

his desk and the professionalism slipping into place. "I take it she didn't come?"

"According to the airline, Mel cancelled this morning. And failed to notify me of the change." Tommy clenched his fists.

"Well. She's done it now, man. You're taking her to court, right? Tell me you're calling because you're going to authorize me to start proceedings."

He closed his eyes. "What's the point?"

"Your daughter is the point. Parental alienation is the point. The fact that she's in direct violation of a duly authorized visitation order is the point."

"I know. But Don, she's connected."

"So we start with a petition to transfer the case to New Mexico."

"You can do that?"

There was a pause and the sound of shuffling papers. "Theoretically. It's not a given, but I'm pretty sure we have cause. If nothing else, opening with that might put her connections on notice that we're aware of them and willing to cause a stink if you're not treated fairly."

"Wait. What? Causing a stink doesn't sound like a good idea."

"Do you trust me?"

Tommy sighed. "Yes."

"Then trust me, okay? Bottom line, you want your daughter for the fifty percent custody you were awarded. We're not looking for a new split—although, I may make them think we're going to go after full custody if she pulls another stunt like this—we just want you to be allowed to exercise your custody without interference."

"What if—"

"Don't do that. There are a million and one what ifs, and most are bad. But we're not playing that game right now. Right now, we're going to file paperwork notifying the court that she failed to put your kid on the plane this morning. And she failed to notify you of that decision. That's two strikes right there. You did the right thing calling me instead of her. You didn't call her, right?"

"Right. I wanted to. But I didn't trust myself."

Don laughed. "Keep doing that. You've made no contact?"

"That's correct." Should he have tried her first? Maybe there was a good explanation. No. That wasn't true. But why couldn't they deal with this like adults? It wasn't as if he was the one who wanted the divorce. "Should I have texted her at least?"

"No. As volatile as Mel is, you're better off leaving that to me. What time did the flight land?"

"About forty minutes ago."

"Okay. I'm going to go. I'll call her lawyer and get the ball rolling. It's going to be all right."

Tommy shook his head. "Can I get that in writing?"

Don chuckled. "Sure. I'll write it at the bottom of my next bill."

"Perfect." Tommy managed a short laugh. "Keep me posted."

"You know I will. You're in town? Airport, right?"

"Yeah."

"You want to hang? We can get dinner if you don't mind finding something to do until five. Maybe five thirty."

This was where Don was better than any other lawyer Tommy had dealt with. The guy cared—and he was okay with being a friend. Tommy could use a friend. "You know what? That sounds good. I'll hit up the mall—there are a couple of new games I've wanted to look at. And there's a bookstore. I'll manage."

"Sounds good. If you're heading to Coronado Center, what about Rusty Taco?"

"Done. I'll see you there. Thanks, Don." Tommy ended the

call and dropped his phone into the holder on his dash before hooking up the charging cable. He should let Wayne know. Maybe check in with Joaquin, make sure they didn't need him to hurry back to the ranch.

He didn't want to do any of those things.

He started the truck and backed out of his parking spot. The gang at the ranch could wait. For now, he'd head to the mall and try to forget for a couple of hours.

TOMMY SHIFTED into park in front of his cabin and blew out a breath. The downside of dinner with his attorney was a seriously late return to the ranch. His alarm was going to go off entirely too early in the morning. Particularly since he wasn't quite ready to crawl into bed. He'd need an hour—at least—before that happened.

He pushed open the car door and frowned. What was Joaquin doing on his porch steps?

"Hey man, we've been worried."

Guilt swamped him. He'd meant to text. Eventually. "Yeah, sorry. Why aren't you asleep?"

"I got up to feed Elise and get her resettled, noticed you weren't back. Figured I'd come out and sit for a bit."

"In the cold?"

Joaquin shrugged. "I have a coat."

And a hat—probably something hand-knitted from the alpacas and sheep that Joaquin's wife, Indigo, had brought to the ranch a little over a year ago. She and Joaquin had hit it off right away—too well, in fact—and now they had a four-month-old baby together.

"You want to come in?"

"Nah. Just wanted to make sure you were okay."

Tommy shook his head. "I'm not. But Don's working on it."

"She's not here." Joaquin scowled. "I'm glad you've got Don on the case. I don't think I would've been able to refrain from kicking your tail if you'd just slunk home without making a fuss."

It had been tempting. But doing that would just ensure it happened again. And again. And again. Until he gave up. It was what Mel was hoping for. Tommy knew that as surely as he knew his own name.

"Yeah, well, you might disagree when this gets going. For good or for ill, I stuck a stick in the hornet's nest and stirred."

Joaquin chuckled. "That's an image."

"It's accurate." Don had gotten a call from Mel's lawyer while they were eating. The man had been all soothing and smarmy—suggesting that Tommy had simply missed Mel's communication about the change in plans. Those were the words—as if this was just a little shift in the schedule as opposed to pushing off the next chance for his daughter to come to the ranch until spring break. Don had pushed back—hard—and now Tommy was set to go up and visit next week. But it would all go sideways. It always did when Mel had home-court advantage.

"Anyway, thanks for worrying, I guess. Go inside before you freeze. I'll see you in the morning."

"Okay. Promise me one thing, first." Joaquin stood and stretched before stepping down and standing beside Tommy.

"What?"

"Spend a couple minutes tonight praying for your daughter. And her mother."

Tommy shuddered. He could pray for Olivia. That was easy. But Mel? He fought the urge to hunch his shoulders. Mel probably needed more prayer than anyone else. Did he really have to be the one doing it? "Yeah, okay."

Joaquin clapped Tommy's shoulder before slipping away into the stillness of the night.

Tommy blew out and watched as the frozen air of his breath slowly drifted off. He rubbed his hands together as he climbed the stairs and let himself into his cabin.

Ahh. Blessed warmth.

Tommy hung his jacket on a peg and tucked his boots under the bench by the door. He tossed his keys onto the kitchen table and slid his phone out of his pocket, pausing to check for messages.

Nothing.

What story was she spinning for Livy?

He'd spoken to her on the phone Sunday night. She'd been excited to see him. Excited to get back to the ranch, finally. When he and Mel had first divorced, Mel hadn't made a fuss about the visits, so Olivia had come down for the whole summer. She'd tagged along as he fixed things. They'd ridden horses and gone shooting together. It was basically three months of fun. Then, slowly, Mel had insisted Olivia needed to be home so she could attend a camp, a sports intensive, swim team with her friends. It was all reasonable on the surface, but the alternate arrangements she'd promised had never materialized.

And now here he was. He only saw Livy when he made the drive—or scraped up enough to fly and rent a car when he got there, in addition to a hotel big enough for the two of them. And even then, Mel found ways to cut in. There were parties or projects or practices and before he knew what happened, he was lucky to get an hour a day on the weeks she was supposed to be completely his.

Tommy dropped his phone in the charger and trudged to the living room. He flopped in front of the TV and fired up the Xbox. He'd shoot things for thirty minutes and then go to bed.

He couldn't do anything about Mel right now. He couldn't protect Olivia from her lies.

But he was going to take the steps he needed to and change things. It couldn't go on like this.

Olivia needed him.

And he needed her.

3

Jade drew her eyebrows together and watched Tommy shoveling food into his mouth as fast as he could. Something was off with him. Obviously, his daughter hadn't come—and maybe that was the whole of the problem—but was there more going on?

Wayne had tried to engage him in conversation and had gotten a grunt, at best. Joaquin had tried. So had Betsy and Indigo and, well, basically everyone. Elise had let him be, and had laid a quelling hand on Royal's arm when he started in. Jade sighed. She'd let it go now, but later, when they were away from the main house, she would take a stab at opening him up. If she'd learned one thing from living at Hope Ranch, it was that shared burdens were easier to bear.

"How'd the interview go, Jade?" Elise glanced over, her eyebrows raised and a gentle pleading visible in her eyes.

So, the tension was too much for her, too. Jade could play along. "Really well, actually. I think it's a good fit, and she didn't balk at my hourly rate. We're going to give it a three-week trial and go from there."

"Three weeks? Why not two? Or a full month?" Royal shook his head. "That's weird."

Jade shrugged. "It struck me as odd, too, but I don't have a reason to push for something else. And three weeks should definitely let us figure out if we work well together. She's already sent an email to a friend of hers, though, and I have an interview with her later this afternoon."

"Congratulations." Elise smiled. "I bet that feels good."

"It does." Things had been getting tight in the paycheck arena—having a new direction for gaining clients was a huge breath of relief. "It's funny, because when Betsy first suggested I pray about finding job opportunities, I kind of rolled my eyes. Does God really care about little stuff like that? But I did it—and even though I didn't get options right away, I started to freak out about it less. And that in itself was a huge blessing."

Betsy grinned. "I love hearing that. Thank you, hon. It's certainly how my own prayer life has played out over the years."

Wayne nodded. "Mine, too."

Jade shifted in her seat and tried to subtly glance toward Tommy. "I've started praying for your daughter, Tommy."

He stopped chewing and stared at her. After a moment, he visibly swallowed. "Thanks."

"I didn't say anything, man." Joaquin chuckled as he stood and picked up his plate. "But I think maybe it's something we should all do."

"Not just Olivia." Tommy's gaze shifted to Joaquin. "You were right that I need to pray for Mel. She needs it. Not just because she's a raging—"

"Tommy." Betsy sent him a stern look before her features softened. "Will you tell us? Please?"

He sighed and stared down at his plate. Finally, he started to speak. He told them about the trip to the airport and dinner with his attorney. Then he cleared his throat. "Don called this morning, early. Her lawyer had doubled down on this being a big misunderstanding. He tried to play off like Mel hadn't realized I wanted her to come here."

"Didn't she buy the tickets?" Joaquin set his plate back down. "I thought you said she insisted that she would buy them."

"Yeah. And that's what Don mentioned. He said it got super quiet on the phone for a minute and then the other lawyer had to leave and promised to call him back."

Jade snorted. "Nice."

Tommy shrugged. "Par for the course. Anyway, it feels good to finally be doing something. Scary, but good."

Joaquin nodded and carried his plate into the kitchen. "Thanks for lunch, Maria. I've got to scoot. Apparently, there's a burst pipe in one of the cabins."

Wayne winced.

"You need a hand?"

Joaquin glanced at Tommy. "I wouldn't mind, if you're free."

Tommy stood and gathered his plate. "I've got time. Thanks, you guys."

Jade watched them leave and waited for others to trickle out —everyone heading back to the work that occupied them during the day. When it was just Wayne, Betsy, and Elise remaining, Jade turned to her grandmother. "Why doesn't he ask for help?"

"Tommy?" Betsy shook her head. "I imagine he's embarrassed. He's been here what, seven years, Wayne?"

"Something like that."

"Olivia used to come out in the summers. Then the visits tapered off. He was trying to turn the other cheek. Be the bigger adult." Betsy sighed. "I'm afraid some of that was on our recommendation. But I don't think any of us expected that his ex-wife, Melody, would turn out to be so vindictive."

Vindictive was the right word, for sure. Jade considered that she had a decent imagination, but she couldn't figure out why anyone would use their kids as a bargaining chip. Her own mother—for all her faults—had drawn the line there. Oh, she gave it a quick try, testing the waters, but the first balk was enough to shut it down.

Would things have been different for Jade if her mother had pushed harder? Would Martin have given in eventually?

She glanced over at Elise and bit her lip. Knowing the rest of her dad's family, Jade was starting to realize that it was better—for everyone—that she wasn't able to answer that question.

"Is there any way I—we—can help him? It breaks my heart seeing him so deflated." Jade looked at her grandparents. "Prayer is good. I get that. But it feels so . . ."

"Inadequate?" Wayne reached over and patted Jade's arm. "It isn't. I promise. And with someone like Tommy, you're better off waiting until he asks."

"Even if it makes things worse in the meantime?" Jade was no stranger to pride, but it still grated. He had people who considered him family—he should let them help.

"Even if." Betsy offered a sad smile. "Now, what time is your next interview? And these are Christian authors? Are there any names I'd recognize? I need to know if my granddaughter is rubbing elbows with the rich and famous. That has to get me points at the next women's luncheon."

Jade chuckled at Betsy's wink and leaned back in her chair. She had three hours before her interview. That was plenty of time to talk books and authors. She'd think about Tommy later. Or maybe she'd be better off thinking about why she *wanted* to think about Tommy.

~

A TRUCK DOOR SLAMMED. Jade hopped up and raced to the window to peer out. Tommy was striding back into his cabin, his lips moving. She watched a moment before giving herself a shake. She wasn't interested in what Tommy's lips were doing. It was a lie, but she was good at lying to herself.

She grabbed her coat and slipped her arms into the sleeves before stepping into her boots and heading onto the porch.

Tommy came back out carrying a duffel bag.

"Hey."

He stopped and looked over then bobbed his head.

Jade crossed her arms—it was cold. Winter in the mountains wasn't something she'd considered when she moved to the ranch from California. "You're off to Colorado?"

"Yeah. Just in case Mel is actually going to let me see Olivia."

"You don't sound convinced it's a real option."

Tommy shrugged. "It won't be the first time. I keep expecting Wayne to tell I'm fired. I take all this time off—way more than the vacation days we agreed to when I hired on. He'd be well within his rights."

"He's not like that. Neither of them are." That was something Jade was completely sure of.

"No. I know. Doesn't change the worry."

"She's probably banking on that."

He cocked his head to the side. "What do you mean?"

"Look, I don't know your ex, but I know manipulative women. My mother—she was the queen of them. If Mom was able to get in my head with extra worries—something completely different than what she and I were fighting about? That was bonus. And it helped her win, because my attention was divided. Look how long you waited to get your attorney involved with this. Would you have waited if you weren't worrying about your job—your place—here?"

Tommy's eyebrows lifted and he slowly shook his head. He

managed a short laugh. "I have to say no. I can't promise, obviously, but no. You're right, my head hasn't been in the game."

"And you probably haven't been praying like you should be, either."

He crossed his arms. "When did you get so wise?"

Jade grinned. "It all depends on the kind of experience you have. This kind of stuff? I know how it works. I know how to play this game. So go. But keep praying. Keep in touch with your lawyer. And focus on being the dad your daughter needs. The rest is going to be waiting for you when you get back."

"Thanks, Jade. Seriously." He paused with his hand on the door of the truck. "Can I text you? If I need a reminder?"

"Yeah. Sure." Jade hurried down the steps and crossed to where he stood. She held out her hand for his phone. "Let me put it in so we know it's not typed wrong."

He chuckled and handed her his phone. "I appreciate this. That last thing you said? Being the dad Olivia needs? That's what I want. More than anything in the whole world, that's all I've ever wanted to be."

She looked up and met his gaze. It was like everything stopped—her heart. Her breath. Her brain. It felt like an eternity before she tore her gaze away and finished inputting her number in his phone. She checked that it was right by opening his messages and sending herself a text. Her phone buzzed in her pocket and she nodded before handing back the phone. "All set. And Tommy?"

"Yeah?"

"Anyone who's as committed to being a good dad as you are is going to make it happen."

He leaned forward and pressed a fast kiss to her lips before hopping into his truck. "See ya."

Jade stepped away as his engine roared to life and he backed out, still trying to wrap her mind around what had just happened. He'd kissed her. Tommy. Had he realized what he was doing? No. Of course he hadn't. It was like a high five between basketball players. Or the butt slapping football players always seemed to do. At least he hadn't done that.

She laughed but couldn't quite stop the mental image of Tommy's hands drifting down her back as they wrapped each other in a kiss.

"Stupid." Jade shook her head. That wasn't happening. She didn't even want it to happen. Why would she? He was nice enough. And a believer. That mattered now. But he was a dad with a messy ex situation. She'd had enough of that growing up to know better than to be willing to take that on as an adult.

Shivering, Jade shrugged off her coat and hung it up. She kicked off her boots and turned. She needed coffee.

"Morning." Elise smiled. There was a smirking glint in her eye. "Out for a little morning stroll?"

"Tommy's heading to Colorado to see his daughter. I just wanted to say goodbye."

"Mmmhmm." Elise took the coffee carafe and jigged it in question. "Quite a send off."

Jade closed her eyes for a moment. "You saw it."

"I did. Has that been going on long?"

"There's nothing going on. I don't even know what he was doing."

"Looked like he did."

Jade snorted. Elise wasn't wrong. Tommy had definitely hit her square on the mouth. That had given her a new close-up of his eyes. She could get lost in those eyes. She didn't want to. Or need to. "Were you going to pour me some coffee, or just taunt me with it?"

Elise chuckled and reached for another mug. "So?"

"So nothing. I just gave him some advice. His ex and my mom seem like they're made from the same mold. He needs to keep his focus and not let her in his head rent free if he's going to do what's best for his daughter."

Elise nodded and pushed the coffee toward Jade. "He's got his priorities straight. Which is more than Martin ever did."

"Elise—"

"No. Let me finish. I know you've forgiven me. And I'm grateful. But I can't help being frustrated that I didn't ask—didn't know—and that unlike Tommy, Martin didn't choose to do right by his child."

Jade reached over and covered Elise's hand. "You're doing it now."

4

Tommy paced the length of his hotel room for the twentieth time in the last five minutes. Mel was supposed to call him and tell him when he could pick up Olivia and take her skiing. She was going to pull her out of school early.

Of course, this was the same song and dance she'd been spouting since he'd arrived late Saturday night. Church on Sunday? No go. An outing Monday after school? Nope. Tuesday and Wednesday? Same thing. Now he'd just have to wait and see what the excuse was for today.

He strode to the window and twitched open the curtain. Snow fell with thick, fat flakes. He shook his head. That would be her reason right there. The snow. Too heavy. Too fast. Too dangerous. It wouldn't matter that he was used to driving in these conditions—they got snow just like this in New Mexico.

Tommy dropped his head against the glass of the window. Don had assured him that staying and documenting—because now when the phone rang, Tommy was hitting the speaker button on the phone at the same time as he clicked Record on the voice recorder he'd picked up—was the best possible thing he could do. So it was what he'd do.

His phone rang. He glanced at the caller ID and switched on the recorder. "Hi, Mel."

"Tommy, hi. It's just not going to work out tonight."

Surprise, surprise. "Why not?"

"The snow. Come on, you can look out your window and realize it's not good skiing weather."

"We can do something else. I was looking at movie listings—there are a couple that I think—"

"No, Tommy. She's not coming. That's that."

Breathe. He took a deep breath. Then another. He wanted to yell. To threaten. To beg. None of that was going to help. Eyes on the prize. "Tomorrow, then. I expect the snow should have ended by then and there'll be a nice new blanket. Skiing should be excellent. What time will Olivia be finished with school?"

"Tomorrow isn't going to work either. She already has plans. I'm sorry it didn't work out for you to see her this week."

She didn't sound sorry. She sounded smug. Which was, of course, exactly how she felt. Don't give her space in his head. That was what Jade continued to remind him, and she was right. "I see. What's Livy up to tomorrow? I'm happy to tag along."

"Tommy. Why don't you just stop? I'm not going to let you see her, okay? Is that clear enough? You can offer whatever alternatives you want. I won't be facilitating anything. You've wasted your time coming up here. Just go home. And stay there. You're not going to get to see Olivia. You know it."

Tommy's grin was sharp, but he worked to keep any hint of triumph out of his voice. "So that's a firm 'no' on seeing Olivia tomorrow?"

"It is."

"And Saturday? Because I'd planned to stay Saturday and leave Sunday after breakfast with her."

"Busy. So sorry."

She sounded anything but. "So when you suggested this week as a reasonable replacement for last week when you were supposed to send Olivia down to see me but refused . . . what was that?"

"Look. Your lawyer put mine on the spot. So he suggested this. I never agreed to it. So I'm not doing anything wrong here. This was never something I was in on. It was just my lawyer letting your lawyer think he had a win. But you know you can't win this, Tommy, don't you? My father knows the judges here. He knows the chief of police. No one's going to enforce your custody order here. No judge is going to change it, either. You need to move on."

He swallowed even as his heart sank. Sure, he had it on a recording, but would it really matter? For all the reasons Mel just stated, it didn't feel like any of this was going to matter. "I can't, Mel. This is Olivia. I love her. And she deserves to have her father in her life."

"She doesn't need you. I'm engaged to Steven and he's a better father than you'd ever manage to be. In fact, why don't I have my lawyer send you termination of parental rights paperwork? Then Steven can adopt her, and you can quit wasting all of our time."

"No. That's never going to happen."

"Oh, please. I can provide her with a mother and a father and all the best opportunities. You're just a bachelor ranch hand. Really, I'm doing you a favor."

"I'm not single." He snapped his mouth shut on the words. Why had he said that? He wasn't with someone. There weren't even any prospects. Jade's face floated into his mind. Okay, maybe there was an option. They hadn't spent a ton of time together. Not alone. But she'd been around for close to a year.

He was certainly attracted. Of course, he had no idea if she was even interested.

"Oh, really. Well, that just changes the conversation. If there's a woman in your life—one you're suggesting could be in Olivia's life too, then I'd need to know how serious you were about her. She might not be acceptable."

"No. That's a no-go right out of the gate, Mel. I haven't met Steven, and you're suggesting that he's ready to become Livy's stepdad. If you get veto power over my love life, then that's a two-way street."

There was silence. Tommy could picture Mel's scowl as she did mental gymnastics trying to get out of that. "Fine. But I didn't introduce Olivia to Steven until we were serious."

"That was your choice."

She growled. "You're really not going to just walk away?"

"She's my daughter. I'm not walking away." He wanted to add "ever" to the end of the sentence, but it seemed excessive. What kind of person must she think he was? And how did she ever come up with that? Had he done something that made her come to that conclusion?

"I guess we'll see. Go home, Tommy. I'll have my lawyer speak to yours."

"I'm here through Saturday. I'd like to see Olivia."

"Must be some cushy job that lets you take all this time off. Are you sure they need you there?"

Don't let her in his head. Jade's voice reminded him. He shoved the worry aside. It was unfounded, as Wayne had stated that clearly when Tommy had checked in throughout the week. "The Hewitts are very understanding. I'm here through Saturday. I'd like to see Olivia."

"You don't have to keep repeating yourself. I told you, she's busy."

"I'll check in again tomorrow in case that changes."

"It won't."

"I guess we'll see." He hadn't meant to echo her words—her threat—but the statement had just come out. The phone went dead.

Tommy sighed and clicked off the voice recorder. He'd send the audio file to Don and see what he recommended for next steps.

It seemed pointless to stay here another two days. Mel was never going to let him see Liv. There was no point hanging around near the school. Mel had put the administration on alert—and who knew what lies she'd told for that—and they'd made it very clear that the police would be called if they saw him again. With Mel's family relationship with the local law enforcement, Tommy wasn't going to push it. An arrest wasn't going to help matters any.

"You didn't see her at all?" Joaquin hefted a bag of ice melt out of the truck, onto his shoulder, and started toward the shed.

Tommy grabbed his own bag and followed. "Nope. Always an excuse. Just like usual. At least this time I have the calls recorded. Don says he has a lot of good stuff and, since I'd told her I was recording conversations, she can't object to it. Not sure what good it's going to do."

"It has to help." Joaquin tossed the bag onto the pile against the side of the shed. "Any judge worth their salt is going to see through it. Aren't they?"

Tommy added his bag to the stack. "Like I've explained before, they're all family friends. Unless maybe Don can use it to get the case moved down here. Then I at least have a chance at unbiased."

"I'm praying for you, man." Joaquin clapped Tommy on the shoulder.

"Thanks. I think I felt those prayers. I was at least able to keep my cool." Mostly. The slip about not being single still bothered him. It was absolutely something Mel would use against him, if she could figure out how. "How's the baby?"

Joaquin grinned. "Perfect."

"Married life treating you okay?" Because his friend and co-worker had married one of the Hewitt granddaughters right before she'd gone into labor with their child, Joaquin and Indigo had a strange and challenging path to love. Backwards in many ways.

"It's been an adjustment. For both of us. But we're making it work and it's getting easier every day. It's not all what I thought it would be—but then, we didn't go about it the way I figured we would, either." Joaquin shrugged. "We get together with the pastor every few weeks, too. That's kinda nice."

Huh. Tommy had always assumed marriage counseling was the last step before divorce, not something people did just because. "Good for you. Maybe if Mel and I had done that, I wouldn't be in this situation."

Joaquin shook his head. "From what you've told me, neither of you were believers then."

That was a point. Going to church—let alone talking to a pastor—wasn't something either of them would have considered. "It's hard not to try to look back and figure it all out, you know?"

"I do. But you have to move forward." Joaquin reached for the last bag of ice melt. "I've got this. Why don't you drive over to the stable and see if Morgan needs any help. If he doesn't, I think we're done for the day. I want to swing by the animal pens and check on everyone. It's been cold and one of the trough heaters doesn't seem to be working like it should. I'd hate for their water to ice up."

"Sure thing." Tommy closed the tailgate and swung around to the driver's side of the truck. "Think you'll have any time to play Xbox this week?"

"Let me check with Indigo. I'm sure we can plan something." Joaquin lifted a hand before starting toward the shed.

Tommy cranked the engine and turned the truck toward the stable. Sophie was leading a horse toward the indoor riding ring the Hewitts had built for her a year ago when she and Royal got together. Now the two of them were engaged and planning a wedding in the spring. Tommy and Jade were the only young people on the ranch who weren't attached.

Was that why he was drawn to her?

He shook his head and pulled off, then parked behind Morgan's truck. If Mel left it alone, he wasn't going to worry about whether or not he should ask Jade out. Life was complicated enough without adding a woman to it.

Tommy hopped out of the truck and wandered into the stable. Horses poked their noses over their stalls and whickered. He paused to rub them. "Sorry, guys, I don't have any apples. I'll see if Morgan can hook me up."

"What am I hooking you up with?"

Tommy laughed and gave Blaze a final pat. "Treats for the beggars. And also something to do, if you need. We finished up early."

"I'm good. It's slow today—well, January, right?"

Tommy nodded. January was always a little slower.

"But I can go get some apple slices. Maria had some going soft that she brought down on her way to the main house. I was going to save them for Calvin, but since you're here and saying the magic words, we might as well."

"Sorry. I'm sure they'll wait. I don't want to deprive Cal."

Morgan snickered. "He'll be fine. He's down here every day spoiling them rotten before his lessons. It's nice that Sophie's around so often and can work with him—he's a natural."

Tommy sighed. Horseback riding was something Olivia used to enjoy. Mel had horses at her parents' place—did Olivia take lessons? Maybe Mel even took Liv out for a ride as a mother-daughter thing. Or was it, maybe, something he could offer? Something that would set him back up as someone she wanted to be around?

"Where'd you go?"

"Sorry. Just thinking." He reached for the apple slices Morgan held out and wandered over to Blaze. He'd wrap up here and then go call Don.

"You all right?" Morgan offered an apple to Cinnamon and glanced sideways at Tommy.

"Yeah. Just this whole mess." He waved it away. "I'm trying to convince Joaquin to set up some Xbox time this week. You in?"

"Sure. Can Skye play? I know Royal would want in, too. He's been bugging Skye a lot lately. There's new downloadable content on the post-apocalyptic treasure hunting game."

"Yeah? Sweet. I'm up for that any time." He'd set that one aside for a while—it was more fun when there was a group of people playing. Instead, he'd been trying to help a group of survivors of a zombie apocalypse get the supplies they needed from various airdrops on the island where they were trapped. He was kind of over that, though. Too many of the missions involved climbing crazily high radio towers, and the graphics were good enough that he got vertigo.

"Here, last one can go to Midnight." Morgan fed the horse the last apple slice. "Then you should go take a nap or something, man, you look dead on your feet."

Tommy shook his head and distributed the fruit. "Thanks."

"Just saying. I'll talk to Skye and see what her evenings are looking like and then text the group."

"Sounds good." Tommy touched his forehead in a sketch of a salute before heading out to his truck. He texted Joaquin that they were finished here and to look for more info on a game night coming up, then hopped in and cranked the engine. He tapped Don's contact and put the phone on speaker before shifting into reverse.

"Tommy. I was just going to email you."

His stomach sank. "That doesn't sound good."

"It's not *bad*. But it's an opening salvo. I think she's still convinced she's going to get you to walk away."

Tommy shook his head and turned onto the driveway for the cabins. "Nope."

"Glad to hear it. I have paperwork requesting a change of venue. That last recording you sent will help. I don't think she's going to be able to explain that one away. Once we get her before a judge in New Mexico, you'll have a better than fighting chance."

"I wish I understood why she was doing this."

"She's got you thinking about her, right? Worrying. Losing sleep? Sometimes, all people like this want is to cause a disruption."

It was the same thing Jade had said. Why did he keep forgetting? "So can you give me the two-minute summary before I go read the email?"

"Basically, she's trying to say it's in Olivia's best interest to only live with established couples, so she has a consistent male and female influence. She's got some psychobabble written up from someone with a lot of letters after their name. Any chance you have a wife you've forgotten to mention? That would make my job a lot easier."

Tommy parked in front of his cabin and cut the engine. "That figures."

"What did I miss?"

"You heard it. That same recording—the one that might get us our venue change? She set the stage for that and I waded in blind, saying I wasn't single. But Don, I'm as single as Adam before God made Eve."

Don's sigh crackled across the phone. "Why would you say you weren't?"

"Because that woman gets under my skin even though I know better, and stuff pops out. Of course she honed in on that one thing and is going to make it her next hill to die on."

"Well. That's not good."

Tommy pinched the bridge of his nose. How did he fix this? "What do I do?"

"I don't know. I think it's going to be easier all the way around if you can get into a serious, committed relationship. Sooner is better than later."

"Yeah. Sure. I'll just do that."

"I'm serious, man. If she can get a judge to agree to her stipulation, it's not going to matter what court we finally get the case moved to. They're going to be looking to enforce the existing decree, not completely rewrite it."

He didn't want it rewritten. What they had now was fine—an even split where he had school holidays and she had the school year. "So, what, she's saying that if I have a stable relationship, she'll stop blocking Olivia from coming?"

"That's what it looks like, yeah. It has her signature on it."

Tommy knew exactly what her signature was worth. "Her signature is on the original one, too."

"I know. But that was before we were threatening a change of venue and she thought she held all the cards. We've got a little bit of leverage here."

"I'll figure something out."

"Serious and committed, Tommy. Two dates isn't going to cut it."

"Got it. I'll let you know."

"Work fast, okay?"

"Yeah." Tommy blew out a breath and ended the call. His gaze drifted to the cabin where Jade lived with Elise. It wasn't fair to even think about asking her to do this for him. She'd say no. But what other choice did he have?

5

"Jade? You have a minute?"

Jade turned at Tommy's greeting and smiled. "Sure. Want some cocoa? It's not the magic in a cup like Maria makes—just the packets of powder—but it does have mini marshmallows."

"Sure. That sounds nice."

Jade shook her head. His tone suggested it was anything other than nice. "I could make coffee, if you'd rather. I just can't have caffeine after lunch or I'm up all night."

"Cocoa's fine." He stuffed his hands in his coat pockets and fell into step beside her. "How's your work going?"

Small talk? Her eyebrows lifted. "Do you really want to know?"

"Why wouldn't I?"

"I don't know. I don't think we've ever talked about my work before."

He offered a weak smile. "Sorry."

"Are you okay?" Jade reached for the cabin door and pulled it open. "You're acting weird."

"Of course I am."

It was a mutter under his breath that she probably wasn't supposed to have heard, but it made Jade chuckle. She hung up her coat and pushed her boots beneath the bench. "Have a seat and tell me what's up while I put water in the microwave."

Tommy shucked off his coat and shoes, and padded sock-footed to the kitchen table. He sat and clasped his hands.

"Spill it." Jade smiled to soften the words as she filled a glass measuring cup with water and stuck it in the microwave.

"Okay." He paused and cleared his throat. "I'm not sure where to start."

"Let's start at the very beginning. It's a very good place to start." She ripped open the packets of cocoa and dumped them into mugs as the song from *The Sound of Music* drifted into her brain. Great. That was going to take a month to get back out.

"Right. So Mel—my ex—got it in her head that I was seeing someone."

Jade glanced up sharply and gave him a look. "Magically?"

Red crawled up his neck. "No. I said something to that effect. She was baiting me. I fell for it. Now I'm in a jam."

Jade pushed buttons on the microwave then turned and planted her hands on her hips. "And I'm the only likely prospect at the ranch. So I'm supposed to, what, throw myself into your arms and swoon?"

His chuckle was weak. "Maybe we can skip the swooning?"

She shook her head. She should let him talk rather than interrupting, but seriously, the guy seemed incapable of staying out of his ex's traps. "She's really got your number, doesn't she?"

He covered his face. "I did well up to that point. And since."

"I guess that counts for something." The microwave beeped and Jade turned to get the hot water. She took a minute to fix the cocoa and to gather her disorganized thoughts. She carried the cocoa over to the table, slid one in front of Tommy, and sat with hers. "What are you asking for, exactly? Seriously, be specific."

Tommy picked up his cocoa and sipped. "I guess just pretend you're in a committed relationship with me for, like two, three months tops?"

"What does that involve? I mean, come on, your ex is in Colorado, how would she even know?" Jade wrapped her hands around her mug and didn't drink. The warmth was nice. Comforting.

"Olivia. This is all about getting to see Olivia. It's Mel's latest thing. She's engaged to some poor sap who hasn't figured out she's poison yet. Anyway, because of that, she hoodwinked a psychiatrist into saying all this mumbo jumbo about Livy needing to only be around secure relationships and here we are."

"I still don't understand what you want from me. Is she sending your daughter down?"

He nodded. "That's what Don's working on, yeah. Since she knows I'm in a relationship—"

Jade laughed. "You think she believed you?"

"No. I don't. I think she figures she's calling my bluff. Please. I can't let her win."

Jade closed her eyes. "Fine. I can pretend to be in love with you for a week while Olivia is here."

"That's a start. I . . . look, can you commit to a couple of months? If we mysteriously break up as soon as the Liv leaves, Mel's going to know it was pretend. That's going to give her ammo and she'll get her lawyer to call my integrity into question."

"Which she should."

He glared at her. "Fine. You're right. This is underhanded and based on a lie. What do you want me to do? Her other suggestion—the one she really wants—is for me to sign away my parental rights so her fiancé can adopt Liv and she never has to think about me ever again. Is that better?"

"No. That's not better." She frowned. Having grown up without a father, Jade knew how awful that could be. At least this Mel woman was going to marry someone, rather than just dragging men in and out of Olivia's life, but Tommy was her dad. She deserved to know him. He deserved to have time with his daughter. "All right."

"Thanks." He reached across the table and touched her hand. "Thank you. For real."

"Yeah, well, you don't know what kind of girlfriend I am." She fluttered her eyelashes at him. "You might be wishing you'd put an ad in the classifieds instead."

He laughed. "I doubt that. Do we need ground rules?"

She raised her eyebrows. "Other than treat me like a lady?"

"I just wondered if—I mean, Olivia might have expectations. I don't know what Mel and Steven do."

He was cute when he blushed.

"We can play it by ear. But we can just put it out there that I'm not going to fall in love with you? You're not my type."

"Noted."

She waited. After a moment of silence, she picked up her cocoa and sipped. "No witty remark about how I'm not your type either?"

Tommy lifted a shoulder.

What did that mean? She watched him as she drank. "Okay, so what now?"

"I guess I'll let Don know that you're on board—I'm going to tell him the deal. I hope that's okay with you."

"Honestly? I think it's a good idea for everyone to know. We're all adults here, and I think anyone at the ranch will be on board with doing what it takes to get you time with your daughter. Your ex is a mess. If she's going to make you play games, then you can play the games. But lying? That's a bad plan."

"That's a lot of people keeping a secret."

He had a point. "Still. I don't like lies."

"Yeah. That's fair. All right. We can give people a heads-up. If it backfires, then it backfires."

"There's no backfiring. We'll just say we're not together anymore. People break up, Tommy, she can't expect you to have a perfect relationship." And saying they weren't together wasn't a lie. Not really. At the end of the day, whatever she could do to minimize lying was going to be a good thing. "Look, my mom was the queen of manipulation. I think I've told you that before. Part of her success was her ability to lie convincingly. I don't want to develop that skill."

"I get it." He reached out and touched her hand again. "I don't like it either. Mel's—well, you never know what's truth and what isn't with her. I want to be better than that."

"You think her fiancé is real?"

His eyebrows shot up. "Huh. I guess I'll have Don look into that."

She chuckled. "Good. In the meantime, I'll brush up on my adoring looks."

"Thanks. Jade, really. I appreciate this. You don't have to do this for me, I know it. But I'm grateful that you will."

"You're welcome." She wasn't sure why she was doing it. He had to have other, better, options. He'd lived here a while. There were probably women at church who would jump at the chance. Then again, maybe they'd think they could convince him to fall in love.

At least with her, they were both on the same page there. She could pretend to date him. But love? That wasn't something either of them were looking for.

~

"YOU LOOK NICE. HAVE A DATE TONIGHT?" Betsy perched on the edge of the couch in the living room of the main house and eyed Jade. "I don't think I've seen you in a dress."

"I'm sure I've worn this outfit." The knee-length boots were her favorites. They not only made the outfit trendier, but they'd keep her legs warmer than tights or stockings. It was too cold to even contemplate bare legs.

"Hm. Well I don't recall it. Doesn't matter, you look lovely. I also notice that you've avoided the question about a date."

Jade chuckled. "Can't pull anything over on you. The answer is tricky. And I guess, at the end of the day, sort of. Tommy said he was going to fill everyone in."

"He did. I think it's an interesting idea." Betsy's expression was serious. "I guess I'm not sure why you're going out tonight, though."

"It was my idea. If we're going to convince Olivia we've been dating long enough that she goes back to her mom and confirms it, we'll need stories. We have a few—I've been at the ranch long enough that it's not as if we're strangers. Still, it isn't the same as doing things together. I just figured if we're supposed to be a convincing couple, we should give it a whirl before we have an audience."

Betsy's eyes glinted with mischief. "Plus, going to dinner with a handsome, available man is never a hardship."

"Oh, Bet—Grandma, I don't have designs on Tommy. I'm not looking for romance. I'm happy being single. Maybe it's what God has for me. I'm praying about it."

"Keep praying. And be sure you're listening." Betsy paused and shook her head, frowning. "Don't let your parents' behavior and terrible romantic choices keep you from embracing the beauty of a God-honoring marriage."

God-honoring marriage. That was a phrase she wasn't used to hearing. Or thinking about. And it should be. Everyone at

Hope Ranch had a marriage that absolutely met those criteria. Even Indigo and Joaquin.

She nodded slowly. "Okay. I'll keep that in mind. But I'm still not convinced that's what God has for me."

"Either way, enjoy your evening tonight. Did Tommy say where he was taking you?"

"The Cantina in town."

"Yum."

Jade nodded. It had rapidly become a favorite. She'd sneak into town for a plate of enchiladas a couple of times a month. "Maria could give them a run for their money, if she ever decided to go into business."

Betsy's laugh split the air with mirth. "She would. Don't suggest that. I'd have to start cooking again. Nobody wants that."

Jade smiled. Her grandmother was a good cook. She filled in for Maria a couple of times a week when Maria had a late night with their new baby, or Calvin needed her at school.

"I think we'd be okay. But I also don't think you need to worry. I don't get the feeling Maria wants to set out her shingle and run a restaurant."

"No. I think you're right." Betsy paused as footsteps echoed in the mudroom and then through the kitchen. "Hi there, Tommy. My, my, don't you look nice?"

Jade stood, smiling. Her mouth went dry. Betsy was right—Tommy had cleaned up well. "Hi."

His eyes glinted with appreciation. "You ready?"

"Yeah." Jade glanced at Betsy. "Thanks, Grandma. I'll see you later."

"Have fun, you two."

Tommy gestured toward the front door. "My truck's out front. I left it there earlier today."

"Okay."

It was awkward. Jade could feel her grandmother watching

them. She wanted to reach for Tommy's hand, but that was a bad idea, all the way across the board. Besides, this date wasn't really a date.

She glanced at Tommy from the side of her eye. "How was your day?"

A smile flirted with the corners of his mouth as he opened the door for her. His hand touched the small of her back as she walked past him.

She shivered. His hand shouldn't feel so natural. His touch shouldn't make her want to curl against him and snuggle in. This wasn't a real date.

It wasn't a real relationship.

She was fine with that.

She was.

Jade looked over at him and smiled as her heart gave a long, lazy roll.

Oh boy, she was in trouble.

6

Tommy parked in front of his cabin and glanced over to the passenger seat. He smiled. Olivia was asleep, her head resting against the window. It was a long drive from the airport, and Mel hadn't managed to get her on the original flight. Had she been planning to "forget" again? Don had been quick off the mark with a call to her lawyer when Tommy had looked at the flight info—since he'd insisted on paying for the tickets so he had access—and saw she hadn't checked in.

Thankfully, there'd been another flight that the airline was willing to change the tickets to. And Mel's lawyer had done whatever he had to do to convince her to comply with their agreement.

Despite the runaround and drama, it was good to have his Livy here. Three days—since Monday was President's Day. It was the longest Tommy had had with her for . . . a while.

He shut off the engine and reached over to gently touch Olivia's elbow.

"Are we there yet?" She might be thirteen—and he was still shocked by how grown she'd looked when he'd seen her walking out of airport security by herself—but half-awake she sounded a little like the tiny girl he remembered.

"Yep. I'll grab your bag out of the back seat and we can go in. Do you need a snack or anything before bed?"

Olivia shook her head. "Mom says eating before bed is how you get fat."

Tommy frowned but held his tongue. It probably wasn't the best thing—certainly not what anyone should do every night—but he didn't like the idea that his teenage daughter was worried about being fat. He pushed open the truck door and hopped down before opening the back door and reaching for Olivia's backpack.

"Is your girlfriend already asleep?" Olivia crossed her arms as she waited on the top step of the porch.

Tommy shrugged. "She might be. But she lives next door, so you'll get to meet her tomorrow."

"You don't live together?"

"No. Does your mom's boyfriend live with you?" He unlocked the cabin and pushed the door open, gesturing for Olivia to go in.

"Course. Why wouldn't he? I mean, we all live with Gram and Gramps anyway. It's no big." She looked around and smiled. "I always loved this place. It feels smaller."

Tommy chuckled. "You're bigger. Come on. Your room's all set."

Olivia followed behind him as he led her through the living room. He glanced over his shoulder and saw her touching the back of the couch and brushing her fingers over the wall. He smiled. That was something he did, too. Almost like a tactile memory jog.

He glanced around the second bedroom as Olivia stood in the doorway.

"You changed it."

Tommy set her backpack on the bed and stuffed his hands in his pockets. "Yeah. I didn't think you'd probably want the Barbie comforter anymore. Jade said butterflies were always good."

Olivia nodded and moved to run her hand over the dark purple spread with the lighter, sparkly outlines of butterflies on it. "It's grown-up looking. I love it."

He let out his breath. "Oh, good."

"Dad. I'm sorry."

"For what, Liv?"

"Mom—I know she's been making things hard and—"

Tommy held up a hand. "Don't. That's between your mom and me. And none of it—not one shred of it—is your fault or something you need to apologize for."

Olivia threw her arms around him.

Tommy wrapped her in a hug. She was a teenager now, so he knew better than to take something like this for granted. "I love you, Liv."

"Love you, Daddy."

His heart swelled. He'd had the creeping fear that Olivia didn't want to spend time with him anymore. That his daughter had agreed with Mel's decisions to keep them apart. Maybe—just maybe—that wasn't the case. He pressed a kiss to the top of her head. "You should get to bed. Tomorrow's going to be a fun, full day."

Olivia eased back. "I get to meet your girlfriend?"

"Jade." Tommy nodded and squashed the tiny sliver of guilt that the fake relationship caused. "She's excited to meet you."

"Do you think she'll like me?"

"She's going to love you."

"She's not mad that I'm here? Mom was pretty sure she had to be made up since you were excited to have me come this weekend."

What was special about this weekend? "President's Day?"

"No, Daddy." Olivia giggled and shook her head. "Valentine's Day."

"Oh. Right." Oh, man. What did it mean that he hadn't even registered that Sunday was Valentine's? "Jade is pretty laid back. And she knows how much I've wanted to have time with you."

"Okay. I'm glad she doesn't mind sharing you. Mom had been trying to pawn me off on Gram and Gramps so she and Steven could get away for the weekend." Olivia rolled her eyes. "Like they spend time with me on weekends anyway."

Tommy's heart broke for his daughter. He was going to do whatever it took to make sure he got to be in her life. No more coasting and trying not to rock the boat with Mel. "Well, you're here now. Which is right where I want you. Get some sleep. Waffles in the morning?"

She wrinkled her nose. "So many carbs, Dad. Maybe just coffee?"

"Coffee? You're thirteen. You don't need coffee." He shook his head. "Let's figure it out in the morning, okay? Love you, Liv. Let me know if you need anything."

She nodded. "Night."

Tommy closed the door behind him and sagged against the frame. What was Mel doing, making Olivia worry about her weight? The kid was barely a teen. She was still losing her baby weight—although there were already hints at the curves she'd fill out as she grew into a young woman. Even so, Olivia didn't need to stress about eating waffles with her dad for special occasions.

Maybe Jade could mention it. He pushed away from Olivia's room and went into his own. He shut the door and kicked off his shoes before getting his phone out of his pocket and stretching out on his bed.

He flipped open his texts and found Jade before tapping out a message.

Settled in for the night. She's excited to meet you in the morning. Can you come for breakfast?

Jade's response didn't take long to come.

Of course. Waffles, right? With whipped cream? What time?

Maybe 8? She's worried about carbs. Tommy paused and hunted around for the eyeroll emoji. *Is that normal?*

For a thirteen-year-old girl? Probably. But we can still talk her into it.

Okay. Thanks again, Jade. Seriously.

Stop it. I'm happy to do it. Go to sleep. I'll see you in the a.m. Sweet dreams.

Tommy smiled. It wasn't going to be hard for him to have good dreams—more and more those nighttime explorations of his subconscious contained vivid imaginings of a life with Jade. It was silly. And impossible. But it did make for good sleeping. He tapped out one more reply.

You too.

Tommy dropped his phone in its charger and listened to the sounds of Olivia prepping for bed. He wasn't used to someone else being in the cabin. But he liked it. It was something he could definitely get used to.

If his thoughts drifted to include Jade in the happy little family scenario, well, it was all fantasy anyway.

He wasn't hurting anyone.

Tommy shuffled into the kitchen, rubbing his eyes. He breathed in the heady aroma of coffee, then stopped. Coffee?

"Morning, Dad." Olivia sat at the kitchen table in an enormous sweatshirt and flannel pants. Those had to be her PJs, didn't they?

"Morning. You made coffee?"

"Sure." She sipped from a mug. "I make it at home all the time. Figured you were probably an addict, too."

"I'm not sure I'd go as far as to call it an addiction." He was grumbling. He knew it. Still. "Are you supposed to drink coffee as a kid? Doesn't it stunt your growth?"

"Old wives' tale. Come on, Dad." Olivia rolled her eyes. "Do you need me to get it for you?"

"No. I got it." He prodded himself back into motion and pulled a mug down from the cabinet. He glanced over at her and smiled. His heart swelled. Just seeing her here, in his kitchen, was more than he'd been willing to believe possible.

"What?" Olivia looked behind herself, then wiped her face on her sleeve. "Is something on my face? You're being weird."

"Sorry. I just like seeing you here. Sorry." He filled his mug and carried it to the table.

She wrinkled her nose. "Black?"

He sipped. "Sure. Puts hair on your chest."

She stuck out her tongue. "Exactly what I don't want."

Tommy laughed. "So. What do you want to do today? There's enough snow on the meadow we can cross-country ski. Or we could take a hike up to the lookout, if you don't mind a little trudge. Or a horseback ride. Dealer's choice."

"What does Jade like to do?"

He wasn't positive, but he answered the only way he could think up. "She likes it all."

Olivia shook her head. "No way, Dad. Every woman has a preference. She might say she likes it all, and go along with it, but she has a favorite. What is it?"

"This isn't about Jade, honey. It's about you. What's *your* favorite?"

"Dad." She shook her head and leaned forward, expression earnest. "I want her to like me."

"She's going to."

"Not if I choose the one activity she hates more than anything else."

"Livy. She's going to love you, okay? I promise."

"You can't promise that, Dad." She held up a hand. "Let's wait until she comes and we can figure out what to do over breakfast."

"Okay." It wasn't ideal, but it would work. Maybe he could figure out a way to let Jade know that it should be Olivia's choice. Or, knowing Jade, she'd already figured that out. She was smart. And she knew how long it had been since Tommy had been allowed more than dinner with his daughter. "Let me drink this coffee, and I'll get started on the waffles."

Olivia groaned.

He glanced over at her, one corner of his mouth twitching up. "I happen to know *those* are Jade's favorite."

"Seriously? She eats waffles?"

"She does. She even double-checked last night to be sure there was going to be whipped cream."

Olivia's mouth dropped open.

Tommy smiled into his coffee as he took a long drink. When Olivia saw that Jade was trim and only had curves in all the right places—wait, what? He wasn't noticing Jade's curves.

Much.

He wasn't blind, or anything, but he didn't think about her like that.

Much.

His smile shifted to a scowl and he tipped the coffee cup back, draining the contents. He shoved to his feet. "I'll get started on the batter. She ought to be here any minute. You want to help?"

"Can I stir?" She grinned.

"You bet. Drink that down and get over here." He winked

and reached into the cabinet for the box of baking mix he'd bought just for this. Waffles weren't hard, just time consuming. But the payoff was always worth it. Especially when there was whipped cream.

After a minute, Olivia stood beside him, whisk in hand.

Could anything be better than this?

Knock, knock.

He looked back at the door. "That should be Jade—you go let her in?"

Olivia hesitated before nodding.

Tommy watched as Olivia turned shy and beckoned Jade in.

Jade looked up and met his gaze. His insides tightened and he could have sworn the air sizzled.

7

Jade's breath caught in her lungs. Why was his gaze so potent? She forced herself to look away and back at his daughter. She was a lovely, feminine version of Tommy. Nothing boyish or manly about her, but it was obvious she was his child.

"It's so good to meet you, Olivia. I've heard so much." Which might be laying it on a little thick, but she had heard a lot. Most of it just happened to be about the girl's mom.

Olivia offered a shy smile. "It's nice to meet you, too. Um. What should I call you?"

"Oh. Jade." Her gaze darted over to Tommy. "That's all right, isn't it? If she just uses my first name?"

"I'm fine with whatever makes you both comfortable." He smiled then zeroed in on Olivia. "It's ready for your whisking genius, Livy."

Olivia held up the whisk. "We're making waffles."

"I love waffles. Your dad promised there'd be whipped cream, too, but I forgot to ask about chocolate sauce." She glanced at Tommy, who stared at her, his mouth agape. "What? You don't put chocolate sauce on them too?"

He shook his head.

"Ah, well. Can I help?"

Olivia nudged Tommy's ribs with her elbow.

Tommy seemed to come back to himself. "What?"

Jade laughed. Who knew chocolate sauce on waffles was such a surprise? "Help? How can I help?"

"Just sit down and enjoy yourself. You want coffee?"

Jade grinned. "As I'm still breathing, I wouldn't mind. I can get it. You two make the waffles. I'm hungry."

Olivia laughed and stirred the batter, getting her whole arm into the activity. She leaned her head close to Tommy's and probably thought she was whispering when she said, "I like her."

Tommy's grin flashed. "Me too."

Everything inside her was warm. Jade carried her coffee to the table and sat, breathing in the heady aroma before taking her first sip.

"Why don't you live here?" Olivia turned, her whisk dripping a big blob of batter on the floor. "Oops."

While Olivia turned to drop the whisk back into the bowl and wet a sponge, Jade looked at Tommy, eyes wide, pleading for him to throw her a lifeline. That wasn't the kind of question they'd talked about how to answer. Maybe they should have thought about it, but they hadn't.

"Um." Jade set the coffee down.

"Wow, Liv."

"What? I'm just asking. It's not like I'm a baby. I know all about sex. I know Mom and Steven do it. And it's not like Steven's the first guy to live with us at Gram's." Olivia scrunched up her face. "I guess he's maybe the fourth?"

"Four . . . your mom has brought four boyfriends into your life?" Tommy scowled. "They were all serious?"

Olivia shrugged. "I guess. How many people have you dated?"

"Just Jade."

Which was stretching it, seeing as they were only pretending to be a couple to score this visit with Olivia. "Some things are worth waiting for."

Olivia chuckled, nodding. "Dad's a catch. But you guys are avoiding my question."

Jade sighed. "I don't live with your dad—I'm not sleeping with your dad—because we both want to wait until we're married for that. You know your dad loves Jesus, right?"

Olivia nodded.

"Well, I do, too. Though I'm a newer Christian than your dad. But even so, I understand that saving sex for marriage is what the Bible tells us is God's best. So. I'm a big a fan of getting the best." Was her face on fire? It felt hot enough that there should be actual flames shooting off her cheekbones.

Tommy cleared his throat. "The waffle iron's ready. You want to pour?"

"Me? No." Olivia pushed the batter bowl toward Tommy. "I'll put too much in and then we'll have to clean the counters."

He nodded. "Okay. Grab the whipped cream and then set the table?"

"Sure." Olivia studied Jade a moment—her gaze almost heavy enough to be a physical touch. "You don't think the God thing is dumb?"

"I don't." Jade stared into her coffee before taking a drink. "I used to. I thought anyone who believed in Jesus—the Bible—the whole thing had lost their minds. I mean really, there's so much more to life, you know?"

Olivia nodded. "That's what Mom says."

Jade could only imagine. Mel really was just like Jade's

mother. She cleared her throat. "Anyway, when I came to Hope Ranch to get to know my grandparents—"

"Wait. Who are your grandparents?" Olivia set plates at three of the places then went back to the kitchen to grab forks.

"The Hewitts. Wayne and Betsy?"

"Cool. They're awesome."

Tommy flipped open the waffle maker and used a fork to snag the first golden brown circle off the iron and set it on a plate. "They are. They're looking forward to seeing you. They'd hoped you'd be here in time for dinner last night."

"Ugh. Me, too. Mom needs to get a grip." Olivia dropped a fork next to each plate then pulled out the chair beside Jade and flopped into it. "Sorry for interrupting."

"It's fine." Jade sipped her coffee again. Jade probably would have wondered who she meant by grandparents herself if the situation was reversed. "Anyway. The Hewitts showed me Jesus in every little—or big—thing they did from the moment I arrived. I—brought some drama when I came. They've never once held that against me. Nobody here has."

"And that's how you met Dad."

Jade nodded. "So many miracles."

Olivia's mouth popped open and she swiveled to look at her father.

Jade pressed her lips together. She hadn't meant to imply that Tommy was the miracle. Not that he wasn't one, or wouldn't be one if all this were real—but . . . oh boy, she'd stuck her foot in it now. There was no point trying to explain, it would just dig a hole. A deep, deep hole she'd never get out of. And this right here is why she'd insisted Tommy let everyone at the ranch in on their pretending, because she was terrible at it.

"Just a couple more minutes." Tommy turned and shot a wink in the general direction of the table. Was that for his daughter? Did she dare hope it was for her? What? No. Of course she didn't.

"So can I be in your wedding? *Not* a flower girl. Like a bridesmaid?" Olivia turned hopeful, pleading eyes on Jade. "Mom says weddings are too grown-up to include children, so she and Steven are just flying to Jamaica for two weeks and they'll get married while they're there. I don't even get to go."

"That's unfair. I'm sorry." Jade tentatively reached over and covered the girl's hand. "Yes. If your father and I get married, you'll definitely be a bridesmaid."

"What do you mean if? You two are perfect for each other. You have to. Plus, if you're not having sex until then, Dad probably wishes you'd hurry up and tie the knot. Steven says—"

"I'm pretty sure that's enough." Tommy carried the plate of steaming waffles to the table and smiled at his daughter before sitting. "Why don't we say grace, eat breakfast, and figure out what we want to do today."

"Sounds good." Jade reached across the table for Tommy's hand. She gave it a little squeeze as he bowed his head and said a brief prayer of thanksgiving for the food. She murmured, "Amen."

"I know what we should do today." Olivia reached over and stabbed the top waffle so she could dump it on her plate.

"Oh yeah? Tell us." Tommy gestured for Jade to get her waffle next, and then took his own. He winced as Olivia blanketed hers in whipped cream. "Leave some whipped cream for the rest of us."

Jade laughed and took the can when Olivia offered it. "It's good, right?"

Tommy shook his head as Jade sprayed almost the same amount of whipped cream on her waffle. When he took the can, he shook it. "Is there still some for me?"

Olivia grinned. "Snooze you lose."

"What she said." Jade chuckled and sliced off a bite. She hummed quietly as she chewed. "Your waffles are almost as good as Maria's."

Tommy clutched his shirt over his heart. "Only almost?"

Olivia laughed.

"No one makes anything better than Maria. You know it." Jade sipped her coffee and cut off another bite before turning to Olivia. "So what *do* you want to do today?"

"Go shopping in Santa Fe."

"Shopping?" Tommy sounded like she'd asked to drag him naked over hot coals. "Come on, don't you get enough of that with your mom?"

"Not this kind." Olivia's eyes sparkled. "We'll get the two of you a marriage license. Then we can get me a bridesmaid dress and Jade a wedding dress and then you two can get married on Valentine's Day!"

Everything froze. Jade's mouth was moving—she could feel it—but the ability to form words had completely disappeared. "I—I—we—"

"Liv, honey, we just aren't there yet." Tommy grabbed his daughter's hand. "We'll definitely include you in the wedding, but it's not something people can just do on the spur of the moment like that."

"Why not? You love each other—that's obvious. I like her, which is the only other thing that matters." Olivia shrugged and dragged her phone out of her back pocket.

"No phones at the table." Tommy started to reach for the device.

Olivia jumped up and rushed into the living room to perch on the couch, hunched over her phone.

Jade swallowed and shot Tommy an imploring look. She lowered her voice. "What do we do?"

Tommy shook his head. "Don't worry about it. She'll figure

out it's not something you can just decide to do like this. You have to plan it."

Jade wasn't so sure, but she clung to Tommy's words like a lifeline. It was easy enough to promise to include Olivia in her eventual wedding when she'd known that was all imaginary. And okay, sure, the girl would be disappointed when she and Tommy broke up—Jade was sorry for that—but in the end, Olivia would get over both of those things.

She stared down at the waffle on her plate. Her appetite had vanished.

"A ring!" Olivia hollered from the living room. "You also need to buy her a ring. I guess you need one, too. But there's a mall. And look." Liv turned the phone around to show her screen as if they could read it from this distance. "The clerk's office is open until five and you just need ID, your social security card, and twenty-five bucks. Easy peasy. Ooh—you could get the judge to marry you if you make an appointment. They convert a whole floor of the building into wedding central on Valentine's Day. Come on, Dad, that's romantic!"

"That's two trips into town in two days."

"Oh, come on, Dad. We'll get a hotel. Please? You were planning to marry her anyway, right? Mom only gave in because the two of you are serious. So it's not like you're doing anything other than making sure I get to be part of your big day. Right?"

"But. I think Jade probably wants a bigger wedding. We haven't really talked about this." Tommy sent Jade a panicked look.

The reality was she didn't want a big wedding. The idea of eloping sat just fine with her—and it would include Olivia, something that clearly didn't happen often with the girl's mom.

"So you can have a big party later. Best of both worlds." Olivia's voice took on a wheedling tone.

"Liv."

She huffed out a breath. "Fine. I'm just saying it'd be romantic. I'm not wrong. Am I, Jade?"

"Well, no. But your dad isn't, either. We haven't talked about this at all."

Olivia frowned and came back to the table. She slumped in her chair. "I don't understand why not. If you've talked about sex —and why you're not having it—doesn't that mean you've talked about marriage?"

"Marriage—generically. Not getting married to each other." Tommy avoided eye contact with everyone at the table.

Jade reached for her coffee. It had gone cold—maybe that was good. Maybe that would soothe the burning in her chest.

"Is it because of Mom?" Olivia stuffed a huge bite of whipped-cream-covered waffle into her mouth. She chewed a couple of times before continuing to talk while she ate. "Mom says the reason you haven't been dating is that you're scared of commitment since she left you."

Tommy looked up, eyebrows raised. "She says that, does she?"

Jade hunched her shoulders at his tone. It was cold and hinted at the steely rage just under it.

Olivia shrugged and kept eating. Maybe the girl didn't pick up on his tone? "She says a lot of stuff. I figure most of it is bull—"

"Liv!"

"Sorry, Dad." The girl's cheeks blazed red. "I forget you don't like it."

Did the girl have no rules or supervision at home? Jade hadn't started the day with a very good opinion of Melody just based on the things Tommy had said—and hadn't said—about Mel. But this pushed things over the line.

"Olivia? What if you went to see the horses and your dad and I could talk about the wedding idea?"

"Really?" Joy beamed off Olivia's face and she jumped up. "I remember where it is! Come find me when you know what time we're gonna leave!"

Jade watched as Olivia bounded out of the cabin and slammed the door behind herself.

Tommy slowly swiveled his head so their eyes locked. Her heart sped up, like it always did when his full attention was on her. "What just happened?"

8

"You can't be serious." Tommy shook his head. He hadn't realized Jade was completely off her rocker, but the conversation between her and Olivia was making him think otherwise. "We can't get married."

"I don't see why not."

His mouth opened, but all the words he was going to say got stuck in his throat. He snapped it shut and stood to start gathering plates. "You're insane."

"Think it through a minute."

"No. There's nothing to think through." He set the plates down on the counter with a bit more force than he'd planned, then turned, arms crossed. "I can make allowances for the fact that you haven't been a believer long, but Jade, marriage is serious. It means something."

She frowned and looked away.

Had he been too harsh? Maybe. But he wasn't going to hare off and marry someone just so his daughter had a chance to be in a wedding. He'd do just about anything for Olivia—he'd jump in front of a train or a bullet—but he wasn't going to marry someone he barely knew.

"You should ask your lawyer."

"No, I shouldn't." He scraped the plates into the sink and loaded them into the dishwasher before heading back to the table to get more.

"Because you know he'd say it was a great idea."

"It is a great idea *in theory*. It is a terrible idea in practice." Tommy picked up the uneaten waffles and frowned at her. "You'd really marry me because Olivia wants you to? What do you get out of it?"

Jade shrugged. "There's more to life than getting something out of every little action you take."

Tommy snorted.

"It's true. Maybe I get the satisfaction of helping you. Or the satisfaction of sticking it to someone like my mom and ending her reign of terror in the life of a confused little girl."

Tommy braced his arms against the sink and closed his eyes. There was that. If he was married, there would be no way for Mel to continue to object to Olivia's visitation. Oh, she'd probably try—because she was Mel and that was what Mel did—but Tommy's case would be a lot stronger. "She just turned thirteen. You realize you'd be signing up for at least five years? Because I'd want her to have the stability here that she's not going to have with Mel."

"Yeah, I get that."

"Five years living with me in this cabin."

"You have two bedrooms."

"Liv would be able to start spending the summers. That's three months of every year you would have to sleep in my bed." He refused to turn around and look at her. The very idea of Jade in his bed was something he could easily embrace. She was attractive—no question there—and so far their pretend dates had been fun. But real life was different than dating. He'd already learned that the hard way once. He didn't want to go through it again.

"Would that be so bad?"

Now he did turn at the vulnerability in her voice. His shoulders sagged when he saw her head cradled in her hands. He moved to her side and rested his hand on her shoulder. The electricity was still there—it was always there—and that was part of the problem with this crazy idea. And yet . . . "No."

Jade looked up. Her eyes brimmed with unshed tears. She blinked.

"If I was ever going to consider marrying someone, you'd be at the top of the list. But I made a vow—to myself and to God—when my marriage to Mel disintegrated. I don't want to go into a marriage knowing that I'm planning on a divorce later."

"Okay. So we don't plan on a divorce."

He drew his eyebrows together. "How does that work? We'd only be getting married to make sure I got to see Olivia consistently. When she's eighteen, we wouldn't need to stay married. That's five years of your life, Jade. Don't you want kids of your own? A family?"

She nodded. "I do."

"With me?" The squeakiness of his voice would have rivaled that of any tween boy out there. He cleared his throat.

"Here's the way I see it." Jade lifted her hand and counted off her points on her fingers. "One, I like you. We get along well. You're funny, and kind, and everything I'd say I was looking for in a husband. We're friends, right?"

He gave a cautious nod. This still made no sense.

"Okay, two, you're a believer. And maybe that should have been number one. Either way, it's something I've realized needs to be up there in my qualifications for any future mate, and I don't really know how to go about adding that to a dating app."

She chuckled. "If I were using dating apps, which I'm not. You get the point."

"Yeah."

"Great. Three, this would help you. I don't think I've ever been in a position where I could help someone with something so important. And Tommy, Liv needs us. You heard that conversation at breakfast. She *needs* us. And more than that, she needs Jesus." Jade sighed. "And number four is probably wrong, but I really like the idea of jabbing at Mel. I probably need to ask God for forgiveness on that one."

"I have to do that every day—multiple times a day, some days—Mel just brings that out in people." He forked his fingers through his hair and studied her. "You make some good points. To clarify, though, it might be a marriage of convenience—"

Tommy broke off when Jade doubled over in laughter. She held up a hand. "I'm sorry. It's just, that's so, I don't know, Westward Expansion. Like your wife died on the Oregon Trail and my husband was eaten by bears when we were building our cabin, so now we're banding together to save the homestead."

His lips twitched. She wasn't wrong. "Is there a better term?"

"No. No, it's spot-on. Sorry. Keep going."

"It's still a real marriage? You'd, uh, move in here and, uh, not into my guest bedroom?" His face was on fire, but it seemed like they'd need to set those ground rules and be clear about them.

She didn't meet his gaze but nodded once.

"And we'd be open to having kids—a family—of our own?" He'd wanted more kids with Mel. That had been one of the thousands of barbs she'd used against him before, during, and after the divorce.

"I want kids, Tommy, yes. I'll be a good stepmom to Olivia, too."

Tommy pinched the bridge of his nose. Was he seriously considering this? "I just don't know."

Jade reached over and touched his hand. "I'll go along with your decision, but I just want you to know I think it's actually a decent idea."

His skin burned where her hand touched his. He couldn't let his thoughts drift too far into the realm of married life—married nights—with Jade or he'd jump into something he wasn't positive about. He sighed.

"Maybe I will go call Don."

"DAD. You have to go away. You can't see Jade in her wedding dress before tomorrow. It's tradition." Olivia pushed on his arm as they neared the door to the bridal shop.

"But—"

"No buts. Go find the tux rental place and get that taken care of." Olivia shooed at him.

"Jade?" He glanced at her, trying to figure out the right thing to do.

Jade shrugged. "I'm not picky, but ask yourself this. Do you want to shop for dresses with two women?"

Olivia preened a little.

Tommy sighed. "No. No I do not. Tux rental is going to max out at fifteen minutes."

"Then go find something to do. We're at a mall. You can figure it out. Jade'll text you when we're finished." Olivia danced in place. "Go on. Love you."

He laughed and grabbed his daughter. He kissed her cheek noisily before he released her. "Love you, too. Call me if you need me."

Jade smiled and leaned up to peck his cheek. "We'll be fine. Probably an hour."

"Hour and a half!" Olivia's voice called after him.

He shook his head and stuffed his hands into his pockets as he strode back in the direction of the mall entrance. He'd spotted the rental place as they'd walked toward the dress store. Afterwards? There had to be a video game store in the mall, didn't there? Tommy turned into the shop, a chime triggering as he passed between the security sensors.

"Can I help you, sir?" A woman materialized from behind a row of suits.

"Hi. I hope so. I'm getting married tomorrow and I need to rent a tux."

Her eyebrows lifted slightly, but the smile on her face didn't waver. "Excellent. What sort are you looking for?"

Sort? There were *kinds* of tuxes? "Um. Just a regular tux?"

The woman nodded and gestured for him to follow her.

Judging by the number of suits hanging on racks and from pegs on the wall, this might end up taking longer than he'd planned. And if the woman asked him too many more questions, about styles and colors, he was going to end up needing to come back with his girls.

His girls. Tommy smiled. He liked the sound of that.

Even though he still wasn't completely sold on this whole idea.

There was still time to back out. They had the license. They had an appointment—barely—for the big wedding extravaganza at the courthouse. He'd gotten Don to agree to come and bring someone else so they had their witnesses lined up. And still.

They hadn't told anyone at the ranch before they had left. It hadn't seemed like a good idea. Which had to mean something, didn't it, if they were worried about everyone trying to talk them out of their plan?

He sighed. There was time.

"Do you prefer a vest or a cummerbund?"

"Is that the waist thingy?" Tommy mimed something that wrapped around his middle.

"That's a cummerbund, yes." She started to turn toward a display.

"Vest. I prefer a vest."

Her smile actually seemed genuine now. "That's always my choice. Much more versatile. You said you're the groom?"

He nodded. "Yes, ma'am."

"Is your bride a fan of color?"

He should know that. If this were a normal wedding coming at the end of a real relationship, he would know that. But no, this was the whackadoo idea Jade had latched on to because his daughter needed them. His daughter. Needed them. Tommy needed to focus on that. He squinted and brought up a picture of Jade. "She wears a lot of it."

"You wouldn't happen to know her favorite?"

He followed her hand that gestured to a rack of vests. A green one caught his eye. He reached for it.

"The jade moiré is an excellent choice."

"It's jade?" He smiled and took the hanger off the rack. "That's her name."

"That's lovely." She reached for the vest. "Now we just need to get your tux. Come this way and we'll get your measurements. You're sure you want to rent, not buy?"

Buy? A tux? He chuckled. "I can't think of any reason for me to wear a tux again in my lifetime, ma'am. Sorry."

"That's all right. I have to ask." She shot him a wink and picked up a measuring tape. "Can you step up on that raised platform, please?"

All things considered, it wasn't terrible. He'd tried on the first style, but the pants were strange—almost like those weird skinny jeans he saw people wearing on TV. When they'd switched those out, he was set. It was interesting to look in the full-length mirror and see himself dressed for a wedding. Again.

With the tux in a bag, he checked his phone and headed out into the mall to see if he could track down a game store.

Tommy whiled away more than an hour looking at video games. They had a decent selection of used titles—he snagged two that he'd been waiting to see on sale—but no one could wander the tiny shop longer than he had. So he texted Jade and headed out to Orange Julius.

He was kicked back at a table, sipping on his smoothie, when Olivia's giggle rose above the quiet rumble of the crowd. He sat up and scanned. There they were. His lips curved. Then he saw the bags.

"Hi, Dad! We had the best time." Olivia dropped her load and plopped into a seat.

"You buy out the store?"

"Daaaad." Olivia rolled her eyes. "Sorry my dad's clueless, Jade. Maybe you already figured that out."

Jade sat with an exaggerated sigh and arranged her parcels more carefully. "I'd noticed. But it's okay. He's still quite a catch."

Olivia made a gagging motion, but her eyes sparkled.

Tommy suspected Liv was over the moon with how things were going. Hopefully, that would continue and she wouldn't notice how carefully both he and Jade avoided saying the L-word in situations where it would otherwise be a natural fit. "You ladies ready to go back to the hotel?"

"We don't get smoothies, too?" Jade pointed at his drink cup. "Shopping is a thirsty job, you know."

He chuckled. "My bad. Flavor choices?"

"Strawberry banana for me." Jade set her phone on the table.

"Can I come up with you while I'm deciding?" Olivia sprang to her feet.

"Sure. I can always use the help." Tommy stood and gestured for Livy to go ahead of him. This was what he'd been aching for. This was his family. And, okay, maybe it wasn't exactly how he'd planned it to happen, but God's plans weren't always the same as man's. He fought a wince. He'd been praying basically nonstop since Jade had proposed this crazy scheme. At this point, he was just hoping he'd see whatever roadblock God threw in their way —and recognize what it was—if this wasn't what He wanted. It didn't sit perfectly well. He wasn't positive it was how someone was supposed to discern God's will. But for now, at least, he was going with it.

"Oh! They have tropical. Can I get that?" Olivia glanced over her shoulder at him.

"Course. What size?"

"Oh. Um." Olivia bit her lip. "Hang on a second."

Tommy watched as Olivia scurried back to the table and had a hurried conversation with Jade. In moments, she was back.

"Medium. For both of us. And I'm supposed to tell you that Jade's going to want a pretzel before we leave the mall."

"Got it." Tommy stepped up to the cashier and placed the order, then turned back to his daughter. "Smoothies, pretzel, hotel. We'll still have time to swim tonight if you want."

Olivia shook her head. "Uh-uh, Dad. You're forgetting something."

He paid for the smoothies and slid down the counter to the pickup area. "I don't think so, hon."

"Rings? Duh?" Olivia rolled her eyes. Again.

"Do you roll your eyes this much around your mother?"

"Probably more."

Tommy fought a laugh. He cleared his throat. "Maybe it's something to try to get a hold on."

She hunched her shoulders. "Sorry."

He slung his arm around her. "I love you, Livy."

"I know, Dad. Love you, too." She reached for the tropical smoothie when they slid it across the counter. "I'm gonna go back to Jade."

Tommy followed her progress back to the table. She and Jade had hit it off. If nothing else, he could rest easy that Olivia was definitely on board with her new stepmother.

He was, too, if he let himself think about it.

He just wasn't sure if that was wise.

9

"You shouldn't be nervous." Olivia brushed her hand down the skirt of the green silk dress they'd found for her at the mall. "You look amazing. Dad's going to flip."

Jade nodded and pressed a hand to her stomach. There were butterflies there that seemed to be in the process of actively birthing even more butterflies. Why had she thought this was a good idea? She looked over at Olivia, who was still chattering away. Right. That was why. In the just over twenty-four hours since Jade had met Olivia, she'd watched the girl blossom. Maybe, just maybe, Olivia was like this at home. But Jade doubted it.

"Can I see the ring again?" Olivia grabbed at Jade's left hand.

No one had been more surprised than Jade when Tommy had pointed decisively to a gorgeous dark green stone surrounded by diamonds, and asked if she liked it. Apparently, he'd had time to do a little pre-shopping for rings and his eye had been drawn to the jade. It wasn't traditional, but it was lovely and unique. Jade held out her hand.

Olivia sighed. "It's so romantic. I wouldn't have thought Dad had it in him."

"Oh, I don't know. You can see the tendency if you look close." Jade brushed a strand of hair out of Olivia's face. "You look beautiful. I hope you get a chance to wear this dress again."

"I'm going to ask someone to the spring formal now." Olivia gave a decisive nod.

"Have someone in mind?"

Olivia shrugged, but the sly gleam in her eye suggested the answer was yes.

"What time is it?" Jade dug into her purse and pulled out her phone. They still had twenty minutes before their appointment. She blew out a breath.

"Selfies!" Olivia took out her own phone and held it away from her face. "Come on, Jade, we have to. Otherwise we won't have any pics."

Jade laughed. "That's a good point. Let me take some of just you, too. I'll want them for my scrapbook."

In what felt like seconds, someone was knocking on the door to the little changing area they'd been assigned to. The butterflies, which had settled, all took flight again.

"Go time." Olivia grinned and wrenched open the door.

Tommy stood on the other side. Who knew he'd fill out a tuxedo like that? Jade swallowed and fought the urge to fan herself.

"Dad! You didn't say you chose green." Olivia stroked the swatch of vest that showed outside of Tommy's jacket. "It matches my dress. Did you see, Jade?"

She couldn't find words. She couldn't tear her eyes away from Tommy. Her heart thundered in her chest as the reality of the situation slammed down on her like the pianos that fell onto the unsuspecting in cartoons.

"Jade?" Tommy cocked his head to the side. "You okay?"

His voice gradually penetrated the combination of screaming and static that filled her panicked brain. She nodded. “I’m fine. I’m okay. Just . . . wow.”

He grinned and everything in her lifted. “I could say the same. Liv, hon, would you take a picture of me and Jade?”

Olivia jumped into action, nudging them together until she had the pose she wanted.

Jade could only focus on the heat from Tommy’s hand on her waist. Her hip. The small of her back, as they turned and looked at each other.

His lips.

She drew in a sharp breath and looked away.

This wasn’t about his hands. Or his lips. This was about Olivia.

Jade blew out a breath. “About that time, right?”

Tommy held her gaze for the space of three heartbeats before he nodded. “Yeah. Don’s waiting down the hall. He brought his girlfriend. They want to take us out to a fancy dinner after—that okay with you, Liv?”

“You know it is. If they have lobster, can I get it?”

“You like lobster?” Tommy shot her an amused look. “That’s new.”

“I don’t know if I like it or not. I keep asking Mom if I can try it and she says no and goes off on a long ramble about how I was a picky eater as a toddler.” Olivia started to roll her eyes, caught herself, and stopped. “I’m not a toddler anymore.”

“That’s true. You’re a lovely young woman. And if there’s lobster, I’ll share some with you. How about that?” Jade touched Olivia’s shoulder.

“Cool.” Olivia grinned and slipped her hand in Jade’s.

A gooey warm feeling wiggled into Jade’s chest. It was different than the warmth Tommy caused—but every bit as potent.

"Tommy!" A dapper looking man in a dark grey suit waved.

"Hey, Don." Tommy took Jade's hand and tugged gently, steering their little group over to meet up. "This is Jade. Jade, Don. He's my friend and attorney."

"Nice to meet you." Jade shook Don's extended hand.

"This is Angela." Don introduced the slender woman standing beside him in a snug, pale-blue sheath dress. "What time is the appointment?"

"Russell?" The woman manning a check-in table looked their way. "Are you the Russell party?"

"Yes." Tommy reached for Jade's hand.

Jade confirmed that the group had fallen into line behind them as they walked down the row of cubicles created out of garden lattice. It had all been decorated with silk flowers—at least, she assumed they were silk—and for a massive room of quickie weddings, it was reasonably elegant.

"Here you are. Congratulations." The woman who'd handled their registration smiled and started back toward the table at the front of the room.

"You ready?" Tommy's gaze was steady on hers.

No. She was *not* ready. She glanced over at Olivia, the girl's sunny smile cutting through the clog in her throat. She still wasn't ready, but at least she remembered why she was doing this. She forced a smile. "Yes. You?"

He nodded once.

Good enough. She looked around and met the gaze of the justice of the peace, who waited for them near the wall. He lifted his eyebrows, the question obvious. Jade nodded.

The JP reached down and touched a phone that rested beside a small speaker on the table beside him, and the opening strains of Wagner's "Bridal Chorus" filled the small space.

Olivia gave a tiny squeal before she walked up what passed for an aisle and shifted to the left. Don and his girlfriend walked up next, and Jade stifled a laugh. Witnesses didn't usually join the procession. They should have talked about how to handle the logistics. But whatever. It was a memory that would make her smile.

Tommy seemed to be holding back laughter as well when he reached for her hand. "Shall we?"

Jade grinned and walked beside Tommy to stand in front of the JP. When they arrived, he reached down and touched the phone, cutting off the music in the middle of a phrase. With about fifty weddings on his schedule for the day, he was probably pretty tired of hearing that song.

"Dearly beloved, we are gathered here today in the presence of these witnesses to join," he paused and looked at Jade, "say your name."

"Oh. Jade Clarke."

"And . . ." The JP turned to Tommy, eyebrows lifted.

"Tommy Russell."

"In matrimony, which is commended to be honorable among all men and should not be entered into lightly."

Jade swallowed. Was she doing that? Tommy's reservations had centered on that exact objection. Except, her reasons for this being a good idea hadn't changed. Don had been over the moon—but then, didn't every lawyer love a slam dunk? No, the time for second thoughts was over. She was doing this. And she was committing to it—to Tommy—for the long haul.

Maybe they could find a way to make it work.

She was going to give it everything she had.

The one good thing about a wedding at the courthouse—and a fifteen-minute appointment—was that the service went fast. Before she realized what was happening, she was slipping a ring on Tommy's finger and promising to love, honor, and cherish him as long as they both should live.

"Now, by the power vested in me by the state of New Mexico,

I pronounce you man and wife. You may kiss the bride." The JP smiled and gave Tommy an encouraging nod.

Oh boy. They hadn't talked about this, either. Other than that brief brush of his lips across hers before he'd headed to Colorado to try and see Olivia, kissing hadn't been something either of them had aimed for. In fact, if Jade had to guess, they'd both been studiously avoiding it. There was no denying their chemistry.

Tommy drew her close and, after a brief hesitation, pressed his lips to hers.

Her heart had time for one lazy roll, and then he was gone.

"Dad. You can do better than that." Olivia shook her head.

Tommy laughed. "I will. Later. When it's more appropriate."

Jade's face heated. That was what everyone was going to think. And—oh boy. It was just better not to go down that road at all. Not yet.

Maybe not ever.

"There's just a little paperwork to handle and then you all can be off." The JP stood behind the table with a pen in his hand. When everyone had signed the license, the man smiled. "Congratulations. When you drop that off at the front, would you let Myrna know I'm due for a five-minute break?"

"Sure. Thank you." Tommy extended his hand and took the folder.

"My pleasure."

Olivia slipped her hand in Jade's and smiled. "That was nice. We should have bought some flowers though. I forgot about that."

"It's okay." Jade squeezed the girl's hand.

They waited by the elevator while Tommy dropped off the license to be filed and let them know about the break.

He joined them and slid his arm around Jade's waist before looking at Don. "I believe you said something about dinner?"

Jade stepped closer, her arm curving around Tommy of its own accord. If a husband's job was to make his wife feel cherished, Tommy got an A-plus. That was a good thing, wasn't it?

"Did you have a good time?" Elise stood on the porch of the cabin she shared with Jade—or *had* shared. Elise just didn't know she wasn't going to be sharing it anymore.

"Yeah." Short answers. Keep them short.

Jade and Tommy had talked on the way back from dropping Olivia at the airport about how to approach things with the crew at the ranch. Finally, they'd decided to call Maria and ask her to put dessert together—since it was last minute, it didn't have to be anything fancy—and they'd just tell everyone at once. Now, standing in front of Elise, Jade questioned their decision.

Which just added to the list of things she was questioning.

With Olivia gone, the reason for her marriage to Tommy was out of sight. And even with Olivia in attendance, Jade wasn't sure people were going to understand.

She barely understood. And it had mostly been her idea.

Ugh.

"Did Olivia have a good time?" Elise came down the steps and opened the back door of Tommy's truck. "Let me grab your bag."

"Oh. No. I'll get it after dessert. You're coming up to the main house, right?"

Elise frowned, but she closed the door. "I wasn't planning to. I've got about ten pounds I was thinking it'd be good to try and shed. Maria's cooking isn't doing my waistline any favors, for all it's a delight to my taste buds."

"You're lovely, Elise. I hope you know it." Tommy came

around the side of the truck, his left hand tucked conveniently in his pocket. "We'd really like you to come."

Elise sighed. "All right. Are you walking down now?"

Jade nodded.

The three of them headed down the path toward Betsy and Wayne's house. With every step that led them closer, Jade realized the butterflies she'd felt before the wedding had been tame and practically non-existent. She might just be sick.

As if he could sense it, Tommy dropped back a little and slipped his hand into hers. He squeezed. "It's okay."

Jade bit her lip and looked over at him.

"Promise." He smiled.

How could he be so sure? Wayne and Betsy were getting up there in age—could this news cause a heart attack? Stroke? Oh, man. That would be just perfect. Jade was going to kill her grandparents with shock all because she was trying to do something nice.

And her half-siblings . . . were they going to think this was some kind of angle she was using to steal from them?

Was she ever going to learn to think things all the way through before she jumped?

"Here we are." Tommy tugged open the mudroom door and held it for Elise and Jade.

"The Imperial March" from *Star Wars* started to drone in Jade's head.

"You're back." Maria grinned as she slid a tray of cookies out of the oven. "Did you have a good time with Olivia? We were hoping to get to have her around a little more, but seeing the sights is always good."

"It was nice for me, too." Jade paused by the island and breathed in the soothing smell of fresh chocolate chip cookies. "There's so much interesting history in and around Santa Fe. Liv said she was going to be able to use a lot of it in a report she had to do in one of her classes."

Maria nodded. "I can see that. I guess you haven't gone out and done a lot of sightseeing since you've been here."

Jade shook her head. She hadn't. Primarily because she hadn't wanted to go alone, and she wasn't sure enough of her footing with her half-siblings to ask them to come along. They all probably would have said yes—if they could get away from their family or ranch obligations—but asking was hard.

"Then I'm glad you took the extra time. Hopefully we'll get to see more of Olivia now?" Maria sent Tommy a questioning look.

"Don's optimistic. That's some of what we wanted to talk to everyone about." Tommy kept his hands in his pockets.

"Can I help carry the cookies into the living room?" Jade nodded toward the plate Maria was in the process of loading.

"No. I've got it. There are already cocoa makings on the pass-through. Fix a mug and find a seat. I think most of us are here already."

Jade bypassed the cocoa. Maria's was amazing, but her stomach was in such turmoil, it didn't seem like the best choice.

In the living room, Betsy and Wayne were in their recliners, their hands casually linked in the space between them. It was such a homey, loving thing. Would she and Tommy ever have something like that? Was it possible when their marriage hadn't started because they were in love?

10

Tommy cleared his throat. Everyone was seated and munching on cookies or sipping cocoa, talking about the little pieces of daily ranch life that he loved so much.

He glanced over at Jade. "You ready?"

She nodded.

She looked nervous. And a little green around the gills. It wasn't that bad, was it? Maybe it was the prospect of telling everyone "Surprise! We got married," and then seeing how the conversation shook out. That was enough to make anyone a little queasy. Himself included.

He cleared his throat again and, after a moment's thought, shifted to his feet. "Hey, guys. I know it's getting late. Ish. We don't want to keep anyone, but Jade and I have some news and we figured it'd be better to tell everyone all at once."

Royal started to laugh. "You fake breaking up already?"

Tommy glanced at Jade. Her cheeks were pink and her smile tight. "Not exactly. In fact, kind of the opposite."

Wayne leaned forward, his expression turning more serious.

A line of sweat formed on Tommy's spine. He glanced at Jade

again and ran through their reasons one more time before finally blurting out, "We got married."

An explosion of "What?" broke out from everyone and questions flew at them from all directions.

Tommy sat down next to Jade and took both of her hands in his. He wasn't wading into this. He'd let it die down and then, if it could be discussed calmly and rationally, they could do that. Otherwise, he was going to take Jade home and let her get some sleep. She'd said she hadn't slept well last night in the hotel room she'd shared with Olivia—mostly because his daughter had kept pestering her to go into Tommy's room and assuring Jade it was fine. Jade had stood firmly in the camp that thirteen-year-olds didn't need to be alone in hotel rooms. Tommy agreed.

"I guess I'd like to hear your reasoning." Wayne's voice rose above the babble and everyone quieted.

Tommy nodded. "First, I'd like to put it out there that I had to be persuaded, too."

"Thanks a lot, Tommy." Jade tugged her hands free and covered her face.

"I didn't mean it like that." He grabbed her hands and held them as he angled to catch her eye. "I'm sorry."

Jade closed her eyes. "No. It's okay. You're not wrong."

"It was Olivia's idea." Tommy paused and frowned. "Of course, she thought we were dating—which you all know, because that was the whole reason we got her out here."

"Tommy." Jade squeezed his hand. "Back up a little more."

"What do you mean?"

"Mel is getting married again. But she and Steven are heading to Jamaica for two weeks and getting married then. While Olivia is still in school. They aren't even pretending they want her there. And Liv loved the idea of being a bridesmaid, so she asked if, when Tommy and I got married, she could be one."

Heads around the room nodded. That was a good sign. No one looked like they wanted to murder him anymore, at least.

He picked up the story. "It was an easy promise, since we knew this was all pretend so I'd get to see her. But then she got the idea that we should do it now, because of Valentine's Day and also who knows if Mel was ever going to let her come again, and I mean, it was a valid concern."

"So I suggested we should consider it. Because, if nothing else, it would give Tommy a better position to argue for his custody. Married is always better than dating." Jade managed a smile.

"I told her it was crazy." Tommy squeezed her hand. "But the more we talked about it, the more we both agreed that maybe it wasn't. So we did. We're not expecting you to be okay with it right off, but we'd like you to pray for us."

Royal snorted. "For your sanity, you mean?"

Skye whapped her brother's arm. "I think it's romantic."

"No. It's not." Elise frowned. "It's pragmatic, though, I'll give you that. Did you decide how long you'd wait to divorce?"

Tommy looked over at Jade. She nodded slightly. "That's not the plan. I realize that it seems like we got married for a specific purpose and when that went away, we'd choose to divorce. Neither of us feel that's the right way to approach marriage. It means more than that. To both of us."

"And yet." Cyan leaned forward, a scowl etched into his features. "Here you sit, having gotten married without telling anyone, simply to strengthen Tommy's custody case. That doesn't smack of treating marriage with the reverence it's due."

"Cyan." Maria's murmur held censure.

"Actually, I'm less bothered by this knowing you went through this thought process." Betsy reached up and rubbed the back of her neck. "I can't say it's what I would have chosen, but I appreciate knowing that the two of you are committed to making something real out of this."

"Are they?" Cyan shook his head before pinning Jade with his gaze. "Are you? Or is this just another ploy of yours? He said it was your idea."

Tommy bristled. "Watch yourself, Cyan."

"You watch out." Cyan pointed at Jade. "She doesn't have a great track record when it comes to doing anything that doesn't inflate her bottom line."

"Stop it." Skye scowled at Cyan. "How dare you? She's your half-sister and since she came here, she's done nothing but apologize and try to make up for her past behavior. You've even gone so far as to say you forgive her, which means you don't get to bring it up and throw it in her face."

"She's right, Cyan." Wayne pushed to his feet. "Seems to me, there's nothing for us to do except what Tommy asked—we pray for them. And we'll start right now. Why don't we all gather around the new couple and spend some time asking the Lord's blessing on their union?"

Tommy shifted closer to Jade. She'd gone white when Cyan had started ripping into her, and she hadn't looked up from her shoes since. He didn't consider himself a violent man, but only the knowledge that it wouldn't help had kept Tommy in his seat. Jade was his *wife*. His family. No one was going to speak that way about her. Not even her half-brother.

When the group shuffled over—some more cheerily than others—and formed a loose circle around Tommy and Jade, some reached out and rested a hand on one of their shoulders. Cyan kept his hands stuffed in his pockets as he glared at the two of them.

"I'll start." Wayne squeezed Tommy's shoulder as he bowed his head. "Heavenly Father . . ."

Tommy closed his eyes and resumed his own prayer—the

same one he'd had on repeat in his mind since he'd agreed to this crazy thing. *Jesus, please use this mess for Your glory.*

When the prayers were finished—Cyan conspicuously silent when it was his turn—everyone took off quickly. Tommy and Jade lingered on the couch in case anyone wanted to ask a question.

"Sorry." Jade looked at her grandparents, her eyes brimming. "I'm sorry to dump this on you. Maybe we should have brought it up before we left. Or asked permission."

"No, honey. While we certainly would have been happy to be consulted, the two of you are adults. And at the end of the day, your reasons aren't so far away from why people used to get married." Betsy sighed as she lowered herself into her recliner. "My grandmother married the boy next door, and I know for a fact it had more to do with her family needing help on the farm than any deep, abiding passion on her part. But when I knew them, they were the most loving and in-love couple I've ever met."

Wayne nodded. "Love is a choice. Maybe the fact that you've chosen to jump in like this will help you remember to keep choosing it. Every day."

Tommy looked away. Love. They weren't there yet. He liked Jade, no question. They had a friendship of sorts. But love? There was time enough for that. Wasn't there?

"Thanks." Jade patted Tommy's knee. "Are you ready to go? I'd like to try and get a better night of sleep than I've been getting."

"Of course." He stood and helped Jade up. He glanced back at the Hewitts, who were, once again, holding hands in their recliners. He smiled. It was a picture of the best sort of future, as far as he was concerned.

They walked through the kitchen and mudroom and out

into the sharp February night air. Jade rubbed her arms. "I should have grabbed my coat."

"Here." Tommy shrugged out of his and draped it over her shoulders. The wind bit through his flannel shirt, but it wasn't a long walk.

"Thanks." She tugged it closed around herself. "I'm sorry."

"Stop. We made this decision together, and I'm grateful you were willing to even consider it. Don thinks it's going to make a big difference. And you saw Livy. She needs me. She needs us. I'm ashamed I haven't been fighting this harder from day one."

"Don't do that. You did what you thought was right."

Had he? Doing what was right had never been his motivation. That much was certain. He'd just wanted to stay out of the line of Mel's firing squad. It was always easier with Mel not to rock the boat. If she'd left things alone, she probably would have been able to keep dribbling out just enough time with Liv—always in Colorado at her convenience, of course—to keep him from stepping up. "It's hard not to second-guess everything."

"Tell me. I'm a champion second-guesser." Jade slowed as they approached Tommy's truck. She laughed. "I was about to say I'd grab my bag and bid you good night. But I guess we're heading to the same place now, aren't we?"

"Go on in, I'll get the bags." He unlocked the truck before handing her the keys. She hurried up the steps and into the cabin. He opened the back door and grabbed the two little suitcases and the hanging bag that held the dress she'd worn for their wedding. It was too bad those couldn't be rented, too. Although, her dress wasn't so fancy that she couldn't wear it to something special.

He'd have to see what he could find that would give her that chance. Maybe for New Years? It was a ways away, but off the top of his head, he wasn't coming up with any other occasions that warranted black tie.

Tommy used his hip to bump the truck door shut and lugged the baggage up the steps and in. Jade hovered in the living room and hurried over to take the hanging bag.

"I thought you'd be getting ready for bed." He cocked his head to the side. "Are you okay?"

"I don't know." Tears filled her eyes and slipped down her cheeks. She wiped them impatiently away. "I don't regret this, but now, standing here and trying to wrap my head around the fact that this is where I live now, it's hitting me. The reality of it. And I'm worried I've ruined your life."

"No." Tommy set the suitcases down and took the garment bag out of her hands. He draped it over the back of one of the kitchen chairs and pulled her into his arms. "You gave me a gift. A favor I can never repay. And I'm hoping that there *is* something in this for you. Or that I can find a way to make it worth your while."

"Tommy." She tipped her head up until her gaze met his. "You're worth my while."

His heart sped up and he let himself get lost, just for a moment, in her eyes. "Same goes. Let's get you to bed."

She nodded and stepped back.

"Did you . . ." Now it was awkward again. He reached up and rubbed his neck as his face heated. "I know we talked about this being a real marriage, but I don't want you to be uncomfortable."

"Okay?"

"So, um, whichever bedroom you wanted to choose would be okay." He turned and picked up the garment bag. That, at least, he knew what to do with. He'd hang it in his closet—there was plenty of room.

"My mom always told me to begin as you mean to go on." Jade hunched her shoulders and reached for the handle of one of the suitcases. "It's been pretty good advice my whole life."

Did that mean . . . ? "The master, then?"

"As long as you don't mind."

"No. That's fine." It was a good thing he'd sprung for a king-sized bed. When was the last time he'd changed the sheets? He winced. If he couldn't remember, that probably meant it was too long. "Do you want to take a bath or something to unwind?"

"Not really. I've never been a big bath fan."

"Oh. Okay. Um. I should change the sheets. I didn't think before we left and—"

"Take a breath, Tommy. I can help with that. Maybe we should make a deal."

"What kind of deal?" He parked the suitcase he was pulling just inside the bedroom door and headed to the closet to hang the garment bag.

"I'll assume you're doing your best, and you do the same. Things like changing sheets aren't a big deal in the long run. But we're going to both end up exhausted if we're spending all our energy tiptoeing around one another." She stashed the suitcase she'd grabbed beside the other and moved to the bed. She pulled down the quilt and started tugging off the bottom sheet.

Tommy moved around to the other side of the bed to help. "That's a deal."

He pulled on the top sheet, gathering it into a ball in his arms, then added the pillowcases Jade tossed his way, and picked up the bottom sheet. "I'll dump these in the washer—there's another set of sheets on the shelves in the bathroom closet."

Jade nodded and started toward the bathroom as he took the dirty laundry back out through the living room and into the kitchen where the stacked washer and dryer were hidden behind a door.

By the time he got back to the bedroom, Jade was tucking the top sheet under at the foot of the bed.

"Let me finish that. You go ahead and grab what you need from your suitcase and take the first turn in the bathroom." Tommy gently nudged her out of the way.

"Okay."

He finished getting the bed ready, unpacked his suitcase, and collected what he needed to change for bed himself. He usually slept in his boxers, but that didn't seem like the best plan starting out. Sweatpants would be a better choice.

Jade was already snuggled under the blankets when Tommy turned off the light in the bathroom and stepped into the dimly lit bedroom.

His palms were sweaty.

And she was on his side of the bed.

She was too cute to move, though. How bad could it be to be on the other side? He went around to the far side and gently pulled back the covers so he could crawl in. After wriggling until he was finally comfortable, he switched off the light on his nightstand.

"Goodnight, Jade."

"Night. Sleep well."

Tommy managed, barely, to keep from laughing. The heat from her body radiated toward him.

There was no way he was sleeping tonight.

11

Jade pushed away from the desk she'd set up in Tommy's —their—second bedroom. They'd been married two weeks now, and she still couldn't completely wrap her mind around it. Surreal. That was the only word that applied.

The rest of the gang at the ranch was, slowly, coming around. Maybe not Cyan. He still watched Jade with his arms crossed, like he was waiting for her to stick out her hand and ask for cash. Or stab him in the heart.

The second one was tempting.

Well, okay, not really. Or at least not much.

Using the other bedroom as an office was working out better than trying to do everything in the bedroom she'd lived in when she'd stayed with Elise. She was juggling a handful of Christian authors, acting as their virtual assistant and sometimes a little more. One author liked to have feedback on her writing as soon as each chapter was finished. Jade didn't get that, but she liked to read and this woman could write. Maybe some of her heroes were a little over the top in the swoony department, but that was half of what made them fun. Getting paid to read wasn't a bad gig at all.

She checked the time and stood, stretching her arms up over her head and sighing when her neck cracked. That was the downfall of a computer-oriented job. She got stiff.

Today, Tommy was coming back to the cabin for lunch instead of both of them heading to the main house to eat with everyone else. Jade had noticed the other couples pulling away now and then and it had seemed like a good idea. Especially since it got her out from under Cyan's glares.

She snatched up her cell when it rang and answered as she walked toward the kitchen. "Jade Clarke."

"You mean Russell, don't you?" Olivia giggled.

"You're right, I do. Old habits." Jade smiled. Olivia called her a couple of times a week. She texted even more than that. It was almost like having a very young younger sister rather than a stepdaughter. And it provided a lot of insight into the family dynamic with her mom. That woman might have been able to teach Jade's mother a thing or two. "How are you, Liv?"

"Good. I'm at lunch now, so I have a couple of minutes. School's a drag."

Jade chuckled. She remembered that feeling very well. "When's spring break?"

"Not until Easter. Ugh. That's a whole other month. But I did wonder if you thought Dad was going to be able to swing me coming to you that week?" There was so much hope in the girl's voice, Jade's heart ached.

"I know he's trying. Don—that's the lawyer, remember?—is working it, Livy. I promise. But your mom has good lawyers, too."

Olivia heaved a gusty sigh into the phone. "She's not even going to be here. She and Steven are going to be getting married in Jamaica. They finally settled on the dates and booked their tickets and everything. So I'll be stuck here by myself with Gran and Gramps. They're okay, but they're not you and Dad."

"No, they aren't. But they're good to you?"

"Oh, yeah. I guess. They mostly leave me alone and do their thing. Lots of reading and Netflix time. Maybe I should see if they'll get me an Xbox. Then I could play games with Dad."

That wasn't actually a terrible idea. Jade was surprised Tommy hadn't already done it. "Never hurts to ask. I'll mention it to your dad, too."

"Cool." Olivia's voice was brighter. The noise in the background got louder, making it harder to hear. "I guess I should go if I'm gonna get in the lunch line before all the good food's gone."

"Eat an actual meal, not a snack. For me, okay?"

Olivia laughed. "Yeah, all right. Love you, Jade."

"I love you, too, Livy. Call anytime."

"Gotta go."

The call ended and Jade slipped her phone back into her pocket. She tugged open the fridge and eyed the contents. The problem with having someone like Maria who cooked amazing meals at the main house and was perfectly happy to feed as many people as were interested was that Jade had gotten out of the habit of cooking. It wasn't as though she'd started out anywhere near Maria's level, either. Passable, sure. But not something people were clamoring to experience.

She sighed and got out the makings for grilled cheese. There was tomato soup in the pantry and it was chilly enough still this first week of March that comfort food was definitely still on the menu.

Jade had just set the sandwiches in the pan to cook when the cabin door opened. She glanced over and smiled. "Hi."

"Hey, Jade." Tommy stepped out of his boots and shed his winter gear. "Cold out today."

"You were fixing fences, you said?" She dumped the can of soup in a saucepan and gave it a stir.

He nodded as he crossed behind her to get to the sink and wash his hands. "Think we got them all, finally. Joaquin's going to be hanging at the animal pens for the rest of the afternoon—the shearer is scheduled to be here after one."

Jade nodded. Indigo had mentioned that the other day and asked if Jade wanted to watch. She hadn't been able to figure out why she would. "It's earlier than Indigo wanted, isn't it?"

Tommy twitched the kitchen towel off Jade's shoulder so he could dry his hands. "Yeah. Joaquin says it's about as early as he's comfortable with, but I guess Indigo's been using this family a long time, and when they needed to schedule earlier, she was willing to give them the benefit of the doubt."

As long as the animals were going to be okay. Indigo would know—and she'd never do anything to put them at risk. If she accidentally did? Joaquin would be quick to point it out and make adjustments. "So if he's on animals, what do you need to do this afternoon?"

"Nothing. Unless something comes up. Basically, I'm on call."

"Yeah?" Jade smiled. "That'll be a nice change. You've been pushing a lot lately."

"It's how things are around here. Feast or famine in a lot of ways. What's your afternoon hold? We could go for a drive, or do something together here?"

She flipped the sandwiches over and studied the golden-brown bread while she considered her afternoon. "I have another two-ish hours of work I need to get taken care of first, but then I'd be up for something. Is it too cold to hike?"

His eyebrows lifted. "No. Not if that's what you want to do. There might still be snow on the mountain as we go up."

Jade shrugged. She was getting used to the snow. As long as

it wasn't too deep, her hiking boots should be fine. "Let's give it a shot. Lunch is ready if you want to grab a chair."

"How can I help?"

"Oh. Um. Plates and bowls?" He was always like this—helpful. Involved. Present. Jade didn't understand why things hadn't worked out between him and Mel. Not really. Tommy was a good guy. Or maybe that was the problem. Mel, certainly, didn't seem like she was a good woman.

"Have you had a good day?" Tommy held the plates while Jade dropped a sandwich onto each one. He carried them over to the table.

She ladled soup into the bowls. "So far. Sorry this isn't fancy—"

"It's perfect." Tommy took one bowl from her hands and smiled. "And it happens this is what Maria was making for the crew at the main house."

Jade laughed. "Really?"

Tommy drew an X over his heart.

"Well, all right." Maria's soup was probably homemade, but Jade wouldn't let that matter. She didn't know a lot about being a wife—it wasn't as though she'd had an example in her mother—so she just tried to be a good roommate and friend and prayed it would work out. "Oh. Livy called right before you got home."

"Yeah? How's she doing?"

"I think her primary aim was to see if we'd made any progress in getting Mel to agree to let her spend spring break with us."

"Don's trying. Mel's being Mel." Tommy shook his head and reached for Jade's hand. "Let's pray."

It was still a thrill every time he did this. Part of it was that it was new to her—prayer in general. But some of it was definitely attributed to Tommy's touch. It did things to her that she wasn't sure she should analyze.

"Amen."

Jade fought a laugh. She'd missed his entire prayer thinking about holding his hand. She said a brief and silent prayer of gratitude for the meal before scooping up a spoonful of soup.

"Did Liv say anything else?"

"Apparently Steven and Mel have purchased their Jamaica tickets. They'll be gone during her spring break and the week after."

He frowned. "They're going when Liv's out of school."

"For part of it, yeah."

"But not taking her with."

"Apparently. Honestly, I'm not surprised."

Tommy spooned up soup, still scowling. "I'm not either, I guess. I just don't get her."

"Do you think Don could use that information somehow? Surely if they're not going to be around, the court would enforce a visit?"

"I'm going to call him after lunch and ask, you can be sure of that."

"If she can't come down, do you think we could go up? At least then she'd have more to do than get ignored by her grandparents. Oh—she also mentioned she might ask them to get her an Xbox, so she could play online with you sometime."

"That was quite a conversation."

"She was at lunch, and she sounds lonely." Jade's heart broke a little more just thinking about Olivia. The girl needed her dad—beyond that, she wanted him. And he wanted her. "Do you ever wonder why God doesn't just zap Mel so she realizes the damage she's doing?"

"I used to. But we have free will, and God is sovereign. Between the two of those, He's not going to make Mel do something, and I can trust that He has this situation under control. Even when I don't understand it at all." Tommy bit into the sandwich. Melted cheese pulled in long strings from his mouth to the plate as he set it back down. "Yours are better than Maria's."

"What?" Jade had still been digesting his easy acceptance of God's sovereignty. Maybe that was something that came with time. For Jade, new as she was to her faith, it still felt unfair. And a little bit mean. She knew God was good—absolutely believed it—and yet there were things she didn't understand. Maybe she never would. Maybe that was the point of faith.

"Your grilled cheese. It's better than Maria's."

Jade grinned. "That's sweet. Thank you."

"I'm not kidding. Do you have a secret?"

She shook her head. "I just make them the way my mom did. Mayo and cheese on the inside, butter on the outside, grill till golden."

He wrinkled his nose. "Mayo? Seriously?"

"Sure. Doesn't everyone do that?"

"No. No they do not." Tommy frowned at his sandwich then shrugged and took another bite. "I'm glad I didn't know that before I knew how good they were."

Jade laughed and dunked her sandwich into her soup. Sitting here with Tommy felt almost normal. It was good.

Maybe the distant horizon that held love wasn't so distant after all.

12

"I can't believe you made this work!" Olivia hopped from one foot to the other while they waited by the baggage claim in Albuquerque.

"Well, it's good you mentioned to Jade a month ago that your mom was going to leave you with her parents for spring break. Once that came out, she didn't have any justification for not letting you come when it was made clear that I wanted you." Tommy smiled and slung his arm around her shoulders. "I'm glad you're here."

"Where's Jade?"

"She had work. She wanted to get her deadlines handled so she'd have more time next week while you're around."

Olivia's lips turned down. "Oh."

"Hey. I thought you were here to see me." Tommy tipped her chin up, his eyebrows raised. "Am I chopped liver now that Jade's around?"

She laughed. "No, Dad. I just like her. A lot."

"Me, too." The truth of the words was less of a shock than it had been the first time he realized it. Now, having been married six weeks, he definitely considered Jade a good friend. Maybe his best friend. She filled the cabin with joy and light he hadn't realized was missing. "She's looking forward to seeing you when we get home. But do you want to grab dinner, first? You've gotta be starving."

"Nah. I'm fine." Olivia pointed to a bag on the conveyer. "That one's mine."

Tommy chuckled at the bright yellow suitcase with a Pikachu face drawn on it. He worked through the crowd to grab it and haul it off. Ugh. Were there rocks in there? "You know you're only here for a week, right? Not six months?"

"Dad." Olivia laughed and swatted his arm. "Girls need stuff."

"I like your drawing."

"Thanks. He's my favorite. I know it's a cliché. Everyone loves him, but he's cute."

Tommy nodded. "It's the only one I recognize."

"You should download the app for Pokémon Go! We could play while I'm here! I bet there are a ton we can catch that are different from what's at home." She tugged her phone out of her pocket and started tapping at it. "Look. There's a Bulbasaur over there."

Tommy stopped and watched as she dragged her finger on the phone screen, flicking an imaginary ball toward the greenish blue dinosaur looking thing.

"Nice. Caught it." She grinned up at him.

"Now what do you do with it?"

She blinked. "You can battle at a gym."

"You have to find a gym?"

"No, Dad. In the app." She touched the screen again and dragged it around before pointing at a spinning icon. "Look. Here's one. Hm. The people who own it are super high level. I'm not even going to try—I'd get creamed. I don't really like battling. I just collect."

"Okay." He was so completely lost, but was willing to go along with it. Maybe Jade understood it and could explain it to him. "Did your mom say anything about getting an Xbox?"

"Oh, she's said a lot about it. None of it any good." Olivia sighed. "She's such a drag."

As they passed through the doors to the parking garage, Tommy gestured to the right. A "drag" was an understatement when it came to Mel. He'd tried talking to her directly about the gaming console—surely everything didn't have to go through the lawyers? Yeah, that hadn't gone well. There were curses and a lot of screaming and something about trying to turn their daughter into a serial killer. He'd tuned out after that and looked for a way to end the call. "Sorry, kiddo. It might be best to let that one go."

Olivia sighed but nodded. "Figured."

Tommy hit the unlock button and reached for the passenger door.

"I got it, Dad." Olivia grabbed the handle. "You know that's outdated, right?"

Tommy opened the back door, shaking his head. "I know no such thing. Respect is always the right choice. It might not be fashionable, though."

"Please. Chivalry is based on the idea that women are weak and helpless and need a man to take care of them." Olivia huffed into the truck.

Tommy stood, unsure how to respond. It had to be Mel. With a shrug, he left her suitcase sitting on the ground and started walking around to the driver's side.

"What are you doing?"

"Me?" Tommy pulled open his door. "I'm rejecting the notion that you're helpless and weak. Get that suitcase loaded up so we can go, okay?"

Olivia's eyebrows drew together and she scowled at him.

"Tick tock, Livy. I'd like to grab dinner and get on the road. You know it's a good three hours back to the ranch." He fought a smile as he watched his daughter fight with herself.

Finally, with considerable ill grace, she slid out of the truck and grabbed her suitcase. She grunted as she hefted the bag and, after a lot of struggle, got it loaded and slammed the truck door.

"Don't take it out on the truck." Tommy started the engine and glanced over at her.

Olivia got back into her seat, closed her door more gently, and sighed. "Maybe Mom's wrong."

"Maybe so." He glanced behind himself and backed out of the parking spot. "Sometimes people do things to be nice. Most men, I think, who bother to open doors or hold chairs are genuinely trying to be helpful and respectful. I guess there might be some who make chivalry into a weapon, but that can be said about anything. Steven doesn't hold doors for your mom?"

Olivia laughed. "No. He thinks the same as Mom. He's going to take her name when they get married to show he's not part of the patriarchy."

Tommy snorted out a laugh. "Sorry. I shouldn't laugh. Oh, man, maybe those two are made for each other."

"You never say anything mean about Mom."

"No. She's your mom." He'd loved her, once. Or thought he did at least. Seeing as how they'd gotten married and started a family, he'd definitely felt more than the quiet revulsion he had for her now. "Dinner. What do you want?"

"Tacos." The *duh* was implied.

"Tacos it is. Sit down or drive through?"

"Let's go fast. I want to see Jade."

Tommy's heart warmed. He'd never given a lot of serious thought to remarriage before the whirlwind wedding to Jade, but when it all came down, he was glad that Jade and Olivia got along. More than tolerance—they seemed to genuinely like each other—and that made the situation worthwhile.

Well, Jade did that, too, but he was working really hard to avoid thinking about that too much. They'd agreed this would be a real marriage—but "slow" was still the keyword.

Slow was driving him insane.

Waking up every morning with her snuggled up beside him was delicious torture.

"All right, tacos and then Jade. With a three-hour drive in between."

Olivia snickered and reached for the radio.

"What are you doing?"

"Passenger picks tunes, Dad."

"Since when?"

"Since I realized you listen to country music and like it." Olivia rolled her eyes. "For someone who insists he's not a cowboy, you sure have a lot of the traits. Don't worry, I'll choose something you'll like. Mom said you were into weird eighties music—her words—I found some that's cool."

Tommy winced. There was eighties music and then there was eighties music. Hopefully his daughter understood the difference between cool and New Kids on the Block.

Otherwise it was going to be a long three hours.

"I DON'T UNDERSTAND why I can't stay here and meet you at the main house for lunch." Olivia scowled at him over the top of her mug of coffee.

They'd already gone one round over the drink. He just didn't think a teenager needed to be slurping down coffee every morning. For that matter, adults didn't either. But at least he was responsible for his own addiction. Jade had convinced him to let it go. She was right. But it still galled.

Tommy took a deep breath and tried to count through the red haze over his eyes.

"Liv, honey." Jade stepped in. Could she tell he was seething? Probably. Liv probably could, too. "It's Easter. I know you're on the fence with Jesus—I get that, believe me, I've been there—but today is a special day. In more ways than one. Easter on its own is important. Having you here with us to celebrate? We can't put a price on that."

Olivia gave a bad-tempered jerk of her shoulder. "It's a couple of dumb hours."

Tommy sucked in a breath.

Jade made a cutting motion with her hand out of Olivia's line of sight. "So what's the big deal if you come along?"

Tommy turned to hide his smile and the irritation with his daughter trickled away. Jade knew just the right buttons to push. She was amazing. He crossed to the coffee pot and poured himself a half mug.

Olivia huffed out a breath. "Fine."

"Yay!" Jade clapped her hands. "Finish your breakfast and go get ready. We don't want to be late."

"*You* don't want to be late."

"Olivia." Tommy turned and sent her a quelling look. "Don't speak to Jade like that."

Olivia sighed and shoved away from the table before stomping to her room.

"Sorry about that."

Jade shook her head. "Please. I was a teenage girl once. I know how this goes."

"Yeah, well, I was a teenager too. I don't remember being like that."

Jade grinned and crossed to the kitchen to poke him in the stomach. "Really?"

He caught her hand and tugged her close. Her body pressed against his and he fought a groan. His voice came out husky when he replied, "I was a perfect kid. Didn't I tell you that?"

"Uh-huh." Her voice was breathy.

Tommy's gaze locked with hers. His mouth went dry. Did she have any idea the effect she had on him?

Her lips parted ever so slightly as she drew in a breath.

Tommy licked his lips and slowly lowered his head. He'd give her time to dodge. This was a step—a big one. And okay, sure, they'd said they were headed here, but they hadn't put timelines on it.

Jade leaned towards him, her eyelids fluttering closed.

"I'm ready. Let's go." Olivia clomped into the kitchen.

Jade jerked away, her face reddening.

Tommy closed his eyes and started counting in his head again before the words that he wanted to say could come out.

"Oops." Olivia started laughing. "Geez, you guys. It's okay if you kiss. You're married and everything. But we don't want to be late."

Tommy looked over at his daughter and shook his head at her smirk. "Look, you."

He shot out an arm and grabbed Olivia, then pulled her close and tickled under her arm.

"Dad! Stop!" Olivia wiggled out his grasp, laughing and holding up her hands. "I'm too old for that."

"You're too old to laugh?" Tommy glanced at Jade. "Did you know that was a thing?"

Jade had seemed to recover her composure, and she chuckled. "I didn't. But I did know you could be too old for tickling. Really, older than three is too old. Come on, Tommy. We don't want to be late."

"No. We don't. Let's get in the truck." He grabbed his keys and followed behind his girls as they left the cabin. So close. He'd been so close to seeing if kissing Jade was what he thought it would be. He'd had a taste at their wedding, but he wanted more.

He looked up to see her laughing with Olivia, and his heart filled.

He wanted so much more.

13

Jade missed most of the sermon. Between watching Olivia's rapt attention to the story of Christ's resurrection and how it was an exemplification of His love for mankind, and imagining just what might have happened in the kitchen if Olivia hadn't interrupted, she had no brain space left.

Praying for Olivia was a better use of her time. The girl needed Jesus. She was so close, too, to seeing it for herself. She drank in any mention of Him like a dehydrated camel. But Mel hadn't done Olivia—or Tommy and Jade—any favors when it came to spiritual things. Liv could throw up walls and make derisive comments just as fast as she'd soak up conversations and ask questions. Jade was new enough in her faith that she recognized the thirst—and the fear. But she also still knew the peace and joy that came with salvation.

Olivia's elbow dug into Jade's ribs and her voice was a whisper. "You falling asleep?"

Jade shook her head and whispered back, "Just thinking."

"Is this almost over?"

Jade nodded.

It was another fifteen minutes before the service ended. When it did, Tommy turned to Olivia with a raised eyebrow. "What'd you think?"

Olivia jerked one shoulder. "It was okay, I guess."

"I guess you've heard it all before, right?" Tommy held his hand out to Jade.

Jade studied it a moment before slipping her hand in his. This was new. Was it left over from their interrupted moment in the kitchen? Had he been thinking about it during the service, too? She snuck a glance at his face, and her cheeks heated.

"Nah. But it'd be cool if it was real."

"Wait. What do you mean if?" Tommy followed Olivia down the aisle, still holding Jade's hand.

Olivia looked over her shoulder and frowned. "Mom says it's all a made-up story."

"Well, your mom is wrong. This happened, Liv. Jesus is real. He died for your sins. He died for mine."

A tiny furrow formed between Olivia's eyebrows. "Who gets to say what sin is?"

Jade hid a smile. The girl was asking so many of the same questions she had. There weren't easy answers today. At some point, there had to be an acknowledgment that faith was worthwhile. Because as much as Tommy—or anyone—might be able to answer a lot of her questions, there were some things about God that were bigger than man's ability to understand.

"It's a good question, and I'm not blowing you off, I promise, but what if we have this discussion later tonight?" Tommy waved to Joaquin and Indigo as the couple passed their little group.

They must have been on the way to the nursery to get baby Elise. It was nice to have friends from the ranch at the same church—even though they didn't always end up sitting together. Everyone else attended a different church in town. There was a part of Jade that wondered if she and Tommy should have switched—would Betsy and Wayne prefer it? Tommy always insisted that no, they didn't care as long as everyone living and working at the ranch was prioritizing their relationship with God.

Maybe that was all they wanted.

They finally wormed their way through the crowd and made it out to the truck. Olivia climbed in the back and shifted to stare out the window.

Jade clicked her seatbelt and looked over her shoulder. "Are you okay, Liv?"

"You really believe it's true? The whole thing?"

Jade nodded. "I do. I didn't always. In fact, I only trusted in Jesus myself in September, but now I'm sad I wasted all those years being angry and thinking it was some sort of scam."

"That's exactly it. Mom says it's a scam. That church is designed to lure you in, make you feel bad about yourself, and then they ask you for money."

"Did you see any of that today?" Tommy shifted into reverse and backed out of the parking spot.

"They passed around those plates and people dropped in cash and envelopes."

"That's true. But did anyone ask for it?" Jade straightened and looked out the front window. She wasn't going to be able to handle the drive up to the ranch on twisty roads if she was looking backwards.

"Not today. That doesn't mean they haven't in the past."

Tommy grinned. "It's good to question things, hon. I'll tell you this, the Bible says we should give to God out of our blessings as a way of saying thank you. Because everything we have—everything we are—is from Him. But no one checks up on it. No one digs through your tax returns to make sure you're giving enough to God. That's all between you and the Holy Spirit."

"Did the sermon make you feel bad about yourself?" The

pieces Jade had caught were full of love and grace, but knowing the pastor, he'd mentioned sin and how it kept us chained to death without Christ.

"Not really. Although the whole sin thing is confusing. If everyone does it, why is it bad?"

Jade nearly laughed. That was such a teenager thought. Was it reassuring that peer pressure was alive and well today? Not really. "It all boils down to God's holiness. Because God is holy, He can't abide sin. So while we live in sin, we are separated from Him and deserving of death. That's why He sent Jesus to die. It's why He raised Jesus from the dead. Because now, there's a way for our sin to be paid for if we're willing to accept Jesus' sacrifice for us."

Olivia grunted.

Jade took it as a sign to let it go for now. Neither she nor Tommy wanted to push. Nor did Liv need to go home and tell Mel that her Dad was a first-class Bible thumper who wouldn't back off. That would no doubt cause more problems for Don to try and untangle. At some point, the money for Don to handle everything had to run out, didn't it?

The rest of the drive passed in silence. Tommy had switched on the local Christian radio station, but kept the volume low. Probably in case Olivia had more to say.

He'd also reached over and clasped Jade's hand.

It was good Olivia hadn't had more questions—Jade wouldn't have heard them. Her body was buzzing from that tiny contact with Tommy. They'd started with chemistry, but their friendship and all the time they'd been spending together had made it stronger.

Every morning, she woke up snuggled beside him, as if her subconscious had shifted her closer despite the size of his bed. It was getting harder to remember the reasons they'd set out for taking things slow.

Finally, Tommy pulled his truck beside another in front of the Hewitts' house. "Here we are."

"This isn't your cabin." Olivia crossed her arms.

"Livy, we always have Sunday lunch with the rest of the ranch family. Easter's no exception. In fact, Maria probably went all out. Trust me, this is better than anything I could make." Tommy pushed open his door and hopped out of the truck.

"He's not wrong. Come on. It's not long. Then we have the whole afternoon—and all of this week—to hang out. And we don't have to do things with my extended family if you don't want to." Jade pushed her own door open. Olivia's resistance was a little surprising. The girl had met the Hewitts before. Although, she'd been a lot younger then. Still, it wasn't as if they were all strangers.

With a weighty sigh, Olivia joined Jade and trudged toward the front door.

"Chin up. You like to eat, don't you?" Jade rubbed Olivia's arm.

"I guess. Mom said I need to lose fifteen pounds."

Jade frowned before she stopped and waited until Olivia met her gaze. "You don't. You're beautiful the way you are. Your mom is wrong to say it. Even if you did have a weight problem, there are better—healthier—ways to help you with it."

Olivia jerked a shoulder. "She says being a size ten means I'm heavy."

"Oh Livy. It doesn't. Size is a number. You're well-proportioned for your height. You're developing into a lovely young woman. Please try not to let this get in your head. It'll open a lifetime of struggle. Trust me."

Olivia glanced over at Jade. "You worry about your weight?"

"I try not to, now. But it was ingrained for a lot of years. I never let myself eat anything that I thought was fattening. And then, when it all got to be too much, I'd throw common sense to the wind and gorge on all the unhealthy things I could find. I'd swing back and forth, using food as comfort and then punishment and neither was able to make me enough for my mother. I finally had to realize that Mom wasn't who I should be looking to for acceptance. That had to come from inside me. And from Jesus." Was that too much? There'd been a lot of almost-lectures this afternoon. Jade made a mental note to keep it light if she could.

Olivia's arm crept around Jade's waist. "Thanks."

Jade put her arm around Olivia's shoulders and squeezed. "I love you."

The girl looked up, visibly stunned, her eyes filling. "You do?"

"Yep." Jade smiled and tilted her head toward the house. "Let's go eat. I bet there's ham and scalloped potatoes with green chile in them."

Olivia laughed and followed Jade into the house.

"Liv's tucked in?" Tommy looked up from where he sat, reclined against some pillows, legs stretched out on the bed, a book in his lap.

Jade warmed inside and her mouth watered. He was a picture. She could see him in that same place in years to come, his hair graying at the temples, readers perched on his nose. She wanted to be here to watch it happen. To be part of it.

"Did I lose you?" Tommy flipped the book closed, keeping a finger in his place.

"Sorry. What?"

He smiled. "I asked if you got Liv settled."

"Oh, yeah. Teens aren't big on the put-me-to-bed thing. She just had a couple of girl questions." And hadn't it been amazing that Olivia trusted Jade enough to ask them. The girl was starved for mothering.

Tommy cocked his head to the side.

"Oh no. Uh-uh. If it was something dangerous, I'd tell you, but this wasn't and I'm keeping her confidence."

He nodded slowly. "All right. Thank you."

"I love her, too, you know? She's so easy to love. Such an amazing young woman—especially when you consider her mother."

Tommy chuckled.

Jade flipped back the covers on her side of the bed and climbed in. "I'm grateful I get to be part of her life. So I guess I should be thanking you."

Tommy slipped the scrap of paper he used as a bookmark between the pages of his novel, closed it, and set it on his nightstand. Then he turned, his gaze holding hers. "Jade?"

She swallowed. He didn't have to ask the questions out loud. They were there in his eyes and hovering in the air around them.

Her belly quivered. Slowly, she reached over and clicked off the light on her side of the bed. She looked at him in the dim glow that remained, moistened her lips, and nodded.

14

Tommy whistled while he loaded fence-mending supplies in the bed of his truck. Jade and Olivia were hanging out with Indigo and learning to knit. Or something. The other one Indigo was always talking about that used a hook, maybe? Whichever it was, it wasn't something he was interested in learning. And it worked out well, since they'd had a report from Skye, via her husband Morgan, that the youth group spending their spring break at the camp had backed their bus into a section of fencing and smashed it.

"You're pretty happy, for a guy who's on his way to repair a fence he just repaired a week ago." Joaquin slapped work gloves against his leg.

Tommy grinned. "It's a beautiful day to be working outside."

"It's forty degrees and cloudy." Joaquin narrowed his gaze and yanked open the passenger-side door. "Is it because Olivia's here?"

Tommy climbed behind the wheel of the truck and cranked the engine. "I do love having my daughter here."

"No. That's not all. You weren't this cheerful the weekend you got married. Jade. This has to do with Jade."

Tommy chuckled and turned onto the rutted road that would lead them out to the broken area of fencing.

"Would you please tell me what's going on?"

"Let's just say that Jade's and my marriage is going swimmingly." That was true. In more ways than one. Of course, it wasn't their easy conversation and comfortable downtime that was keeping the smile on his face today. But it could be.

Joaquin shook his head. "Dude."

"What?" Why was there censure in his friend's voice? Tommy looked over and frowned. "Spit it out."

"You've got a fake marriage, and you slept with her?"

"It's not a fake marriage." Was that what people thought? Hadn't they explained this? "The marriage is real. Our intention has been—from day one, mind you—to work to make it a lasting, God-honoring marriage. Just because it started out to help me with getting Mel to let me see Liv doesn't mean we aren't actually married. And I find it a little rich that you're going to lecture me about any of this."

"I don't recall lecturing. I asked a question." Joaquin turned to look out the window.

"Yeah, well, it was out of line." His good mood had evaporated. When he stopped in front of the mangled fence, Tommy decided maybe that was a good thing, because the damage here would have popped any happiness bubble in existence. "How does someone manage that kind of fence carnage without noticing?"

"Skye said they had a school bus."

Maybe that made a difference. Those were harder to steer—especially if the person behind the wheel wasn't really supposed to be driving it. "Yeah, I guess. I'm not sure I brought enough to fix it."

"Let's get started and see. Maybe we can salvage some of it."

It was a reasonable idea. Though looking at the broken posts and rails strewn around, he didn't have a lot of hope. They were going to have to clear it all down and start over. "Do we even know why we need a fence here? It's not like we're separating this area from someone else's property. The Hewitts own the whole mesa."

Joaquin shrugged. "You can ask Wayne, but I've always been more of a 'do as you're asked' kind of employee."

Tommy scowled. He wasn't trying to buck the system or get out of work. He just liked to imagine that the work he did had a point. "Seems to me it's worth mentioning. This is the third time we've rebuilt this fence section this year."

"Fourth."

"That just makes it worse. If he needs the fence, great, then maybe he needs to rethink where visitors are allowed to drive."

Joaquin frowned thoughtfully. "That's not a bad idea. I don't actually know why anyone would be out here with a vehicle if they weren't from the ranch. Let's walk a bit toward the lodge and see what we see."

Putting off the fence work was never going to be a bad plan in Tommy's mind. He fell into step beside his friend. "You really think exploring the full benefits of our marriage was a mistake?"

Joaquin's lips twitched in what might've been a smile. "Listen to you. Should we find a couch and a notepad?"

Tommy snorted and jabbed his elbow into Joaquin's side. "C'mon, man. Be serious."

"No. I guess I don't. Not if the two of you are actually serious about it."

"We said we were. At the very start."

"Yeah, but that was shortly after telling us that you were going to pretend to be dating. It was a big switch."

Tommy nodded slowly. "Okay. I guess I see that. You weren't there for all the conversations."

"No. We weren't. And we never will be. That's the thing—

your relationship is between the two of you. I'm sorry I commented on it, because it's not my job." Joaquin stopped and propped his hands on his hips as he looked at the main parking area by the lodge. "This is a tiny, bumpy dirt road. Why *does* anyone drive down it? Especially with a bus?"

"There's room to turn around in the parking lot." Tommy blew out a breath. "Want to go find Skye? She might have an idea."

"Yeah. Let's do that. 'Cause despite ragging you about it, I'm not excited about having to keep rebuilding that fence either. Even if we do have it down to a science."

Tommy laughed. That they did.

The two of them climbed the steps to the lodge side-by-side before tromping into the building. The public sitting and dining rooms were empty—not unexpected at this point in the morning.

"She's probably in the office." Joaquin lifted his chin in the direction of the back corner.

Unless she was doing housekeeping duties or had gone on an activity with the group or . . . there were a ton of other possibilities. But the office was the next logical place to look.

They made their way past the kitchen to the small room Skye had taken over for the operations center of the camp. She'd definitely found her niche here at the ranch—both she and the camp were thriving.

"Yes. We can absolutely do August and September for you." Skye paused. The phone was held to her ear and she swiveled back and forth in her chair. When she saw them, she held up a finger and grinned.

"Guess you were right." Tommy whispered as he and Joaquin moved down the hall a bit so they weren't eavesdropping on her conversation or making noise that would distract her. "But not about everything."

"Oh?"

"You're my best friend, man. Basically family. Everyone at the ranch is basically family. That gives you the right to comment and have opinions on my life. I might not always agree, but I do want you to tell me. If you—and others—hadn't pushed me to do better by Olivia, I might have walked away. The idea of signing away my rights was heartbreaking, but dealing with Mel was—is—so exhausting, it was tempting, I won't lie." Tommy shoved his hands in his pockets. He wasn't proud of that. The idea that, even for the briefest instant, he'd been willing to consider walking away from Livy didn't say a lot for him as a dad. Or as a person.

"Don't beat yourself up. The kind of abuse you've suffered at that woman's hands would break anyone. But you didn't stay broken." Joaquin gave his shoulder a light punch. "That counts for a lot. And Jade? She's great. Indigo and I are both praying you can make this work. Not just because of Olivia, but because marriage matters."

It did. He'd said it to Jade before they jumped in. He still had little niggles of misgivings about how they'd gone about this, if he was honest with himself. He just quickly squashed them, because he'd made a decision. That would be enough—it had to be enough, didn't it?—to get him by. "Thanks."

Skye poked her head out of the office and grinned. "What brings two strapping men my way today?"

"Strapping married men." Joaquin teased. "Who are friends of your husband."

She laughed. "Details. Is this about the fence?"

"Yeah." Tommy smiled. Skye was probably the easiest of the Hewitt grandchildren to get along with—was that because she'd been the first to stay? Technically, Cyan had showed up first, but then his work had called him away and, while he was gone, Skye had come. She'd charmed Morgan right out of the gate, and that had been that.

"Step into my office." Skye disappeared back through the doorway.

Tommy and Joaquin followed, then each of them leaned against the wall on either side of the door. There weren't chairs—the room simply wasn't big enough for more than Skye's workplace.

"So? The fence? I'm really sorry about that."

"We were wondering," Tommy wiggled his thumb to indicate Joaquin and himself, "why anyone was driving down that way to start with. Do you know?"

"I don't. Sorry."

"So, the next question is—if we rigged a simple obstacle to block access—maybe just a chain across with posts on either side. Or planters? Something easy to move when someone from the ranch needed the road. Would that be okay?" Tommy could see a couple of different ways to rig up a blockade of sorts that wouldn't be a big inconvenience when he or Joaquin needed to go that way. And most of the time, it was the two of them who used the road anyway. "Or should we ask Wayne?"

"I don't have an issue with it, but probably. Hang on and I'll give him a call." Skye punched in a number on her phone then tapped the speaker button. It rang once before Wayne answered.

"Hi there, honey. How's the camp?"

Skye's cheeks pinked up prettily. "It's good, Grandpa. Tommy and Joaquin are here—you heard about the fence?"

Wayne sighed. "Yes, I did. They were trying to say we were liable for the damage to their bus. I told them that was fine, they'd be liable for the damage to the fence. We agreed, eventually, that we were probably square. Especially considering the man driving the bus doesn't actually have his CDL."

Well, that explained that. Why would a church let someone

without a commercial driver's license operate a school bus? That seemed irresponsible all around. Tommy shook his head.

Skye jumped in before either of them could speak. "The guys were wondering if they could block the road. Something easy to move when we need it, but solid enough to deter wandering campers?"

"I don't see why not. It's a good idea. Now that we're doing more with the camp—and that's all you, Skye. You've been a big blessing taking that over. It makes sense to do what we can to keep people where they're supposed to be. And since Tommy and Joaquin are the ones who are up there most often, if it works for them, the rest of us will deal. Great idea, guys."

"Thanks, Wayne." Joaquin shot Tommy a thumbs-up.

"Before you go, Grandpa, there's one more thing. Actually, guys, if you'd stay too, I'd appreciate it."

Tommy raised his eyebrows but shrugged. "Sure."

Skye nodded her thanks. "I just got off the phone with a missionary—or he's retired but still helps out the agency with training and problem solving. Something like that. Anyway, he's been looking for a place to do two-to-three months of two-week intensives with potential missionaries."

"What's a potential missionary?" Joaquin blurted the question then hunched his shoulders. "Sorry."

"No. It's a good question. I was wondering myself." Wayne chuckled.

"Someone who is thinking of entering the mission field, I believe. He talked a lot about it and, to be honest, I kind of tuned out. Point being, he's hoping we'd be able to accommodate him for that timeframe."

"Well, that's up to you, Skye. You've got the schedule." Wayne cleared his throat. "You know Betsy and I love any group that loves Jesus. If the mission agency isn't kooky, it's fine."

Skye laughed. "Oh, no, it's a good one. Um. He asked about

building some temporary structures—maybe a simple obstacle course and some stations for typical activities they might have to do in a remote village. That's why I wanted to ask Tommy and Joaquin, as well as you. It's not something anyone's asked before, and I wanted to be sure."

"It's fine with me as long as it can come down when they're gone. Unless it ends up being something the camp could enjoy afterward." Wayne hummed quietly. "Maybe I ought to talk to him and see what he has in mind. Easier to build it to last starting out if we think it's a good addition."

"Okay. And I guess maybe include the guys?" Skye arched her eyebrows at Tommy and Joaquin.

Tommy shook his head. "I don't know if you need to do that. We can figure most anything out—especially if he has plans already or can point us to something online."

Joaquin nodded assent.

"Okay. I'll email you his contact info, Grandpa. The dates are no problem as long as we lock them in soon so I know when people will start to call."

"He wants the whole camp? Do we have regulars who'll be inconvenienced?"

"Yes, and not really. The big August group already called asking about moving into July."

"Okay. That sounds good. I'll give him a shout and we'll get it settled. Bye, hon."

"Bye, Grandpa." Skye hit the button to end the call. "Guess you're good to go with your blockade. I really am sorry about the fence."

Joaquin shrugged. "We'll get it fixed. Thanks, Skye."

Tommy gave a wave. "Yeah, thanks."

He followed Joaquin down the hall. Potential missionaries. That was a new one. But building an obstacle course could be fun.

"What do you think? Posts and a chain or planters?"

Tommy studied the space. "Posts. They're less likely to be ignored."

Joaquin laughed. "True. Think you have enough in the truck for that and the fence?"

Tommy wasn't sure he had enough in the truck for the fence on its own. "Probably not. But if we're going to have to go back and get more supplies, might as well start with this so the bus doesn't make a return and take out more fencing."

"Good point. Why don't you drive up closer so we don't have to haul things?"

"Sure." Tommy started back to the truck. He slipped his phone out of his pocket and tapped out a quick text to Jade, letting her know this was going to take longer than expected.

Within seconds, he got a reply of a thumbs-up and kissy face emoji.

He grinned and sent her the same. Blowing a kiss via his phone was a far cry from what he'd like to do. But for now, it was enough.

15

Jade's jaw clenched as she struggled to poke the knitting needle through the loop on the other needle without having them all slip off—again. There! No, wait. Darn it, she'd gone through the yarn, not under it. "I don't think I'm cut out for this."

Indigo smiled and switched to the seat beside her. "It takes time."

Jade looked pointedly over at Olivia, who was knitting away like she'd been born with needles in her hand. "You started trying to teach me this almost a year ago."

"Well. It *can* take time. Some people are naturals." Indigo chuckled and reached for the needles. "You've got very tight stitches. That's part of the problem."

"If I don't make them tight, they all slip off." Jade frowned at the handful of rows hanging underneath the needles. "I have to start over again, don't I?"

"You don't *have* to." Indigo bit her lip.

"But you would." Jade sighed and took the knitting back. She slid the stitches off the needles and started tugging on the loose end. The stitches snapped merrily into straight yarn. "At least

I'm good at this. If you ever need a professional knitting undoer, gimme a call."

Olivia laughed. "You're not doing badly, Jade. I do this with Gran."

"You didn't say anything." Jade kept pulling out stitches. "We didn't have to do this."

"No, it's fun. And Gran just uses the polyester yarn that's less than a dollar a pound. This is so much nicer. Are you sure I can't buy it from you, Indigo?" Olivia looked down at her handwork. "I have some money with me."

"Absolutely not. Maybe if you want to try a sweater sometime, we'll work something out. How about that?" Indigo picked up Jade's ball of yarn and started wrapping it back up.

"Okay. I never thought about making a sweater. That seems hard."

"It can be, but there are some good beginner patterns. I've actually been thinking of writing my own beginner pattern that isn't as plain as some of them are. You'd be a good test knitter. If I do, would you be interested?"

Olivia's face lit up and she nodded vigorously.

Jade looked at her half-sister. Had she really been thinking of doing it? Or was it just another person falling in love with Olivia and looking for ways to do something kind for her? It didn't matter. But it was a question.

"Time to cast on." Indigo smiled brightly.

"Again." Jade sighed and measured out the stitches on her needle. After a moment of thought, and under Indigo's watchful eye, she slowly managed to get a new row of stitches onto her needle.

"Those look great. Just the right tension. Keep that up." Indigo cocked her head to the side. "I think I hear baby Elise. I'll be right back."

Did they call her baby Elise even when Elise wasn't around? Maybe it was habit at this point.

Indigo returned with the baby. The little girl blinked owlishly before burying her face in her mother's neck. Indigo patted her and put a little bounce in her step. "She wakes up hard."

"I know how that is." Jade chuckled. This morning, in particular, had been a struggle to get out of bed—she would have loved to have stayed snuggled in Tommy's arms all day. Her cheeks burned.

Indigo's eyebrows lifted. Her gaze darted to Olivia then to Jade and she frowned slightly.

Jade looked down at her knitting, grateful Olivia was in the room, because it was obvious Indigo had questions. It was fine. There was nothing wrong with what they'd done—she and Tommy were married. They were planning to stay married.

She loved him.

Wait, what? Where had that come from? Love? Her hands stilled and she closed her eyes.

"You okay?" Indigo sat on the couch beside Jade.

"Yeah. Of course." She set her knitting aside and held out her hands. "Can I hold her?"

Eight-month-old baby Elise studied Jade before throwing her weight towards her.

Indigo laughed and passed the girl. "Looks like that's a yes."

Jade settled Elise on her lap and breathed in the baby powder and sunshine smell that babies seemed to carry with them everywhere. "You're waking up now, aren't you?"

Elise babbled happily.

"She's a happy girl." Indigo stroked the baby's cheek. She glanced over at Olivia. "You okay?"

Liv shrugged and looked down at her knitting.

Jade caught a glimpse of a scowl before Olivia's hair fell,

forming a curtain. Was that just teenager angst coming out? There'd been so little of that so far, but it wasn't unexpected. Tommy had warned her to expect adjustment difficulties with this longer visit. It made sense. Jade had never loved the first longer exposures to any of her mother's boyfriends. But if Olivia didn't want to talk, Jade wasn't going to push.

Elise wriggled and kicked her legs.

Jade shifted so the little girl was standing. "Such a strong girl. You're going to be walking before your mom knows what to do about it."

"Oh, don't remind me. She's growing so fast." Indigo watched her daughter, love beaming out of her eyes. "I was telling Joaquin I already want another one."

"Already? She's not even a year old yet."

"I know." Indigo laughed. "It's insane. He wants to wait until at least August. And I get it. But still. Have you and Tommy talked about it at all?"

Jade caught movement out of the corner of her eye. Olivia was interested in the answer, it seemed. "No. Not yet. Eventually, for sure, but there's no rush, right?"

"Don't ask me." Indigo laughed again, and Elise giggled and drooled. Indigo popped out of her seat. "Let me get you a burp cloth. I'm always forgetting, because I don't care about my clothes."

"It's fine. It's just drool." Jade wiped the baby spit with her thumb then rubbed it on her jeans. But she took the cloth when Indigo offered it. "What about Cyan and Maria? Any idea there?"

Indigo shook her head. "Cyan's always been hard to read. I mean, we have a big family, so it can go either way. Maybe he loved it and he can't wait to add more. Or maybe he's a big fan of the smaller crew."

"Maria gets a say in that." Jade made silly faces at Elise, sparking off more laughter.

"Of course." Indigo reached out, and Elise wrapped her chubby hand around Indigo's finger.

"Calvin should, too." Olivia mumbled.

Jade's eyebrows lifted. "You're not wrong, Liv. Calvin should at least get to say how he feels, although he seems to love his baby sister, so he's probably on board. Will you be upset if your dad and I want to have kids?"

Olivia looked up, her eyes shining. "No. Not you guys."

A light bulb went off. "Your mom's expecting."

Olivia nodded.

Why was that different? Jade couldn't figure it out, but it wasn't something she could ask—was it? She dug deep, looking for a way to draw her stepdaughter into conversation without being pushy. "Does it bother you?"

The look Olivia gave her clearly said, "Duh," even though she didn't use the word.

Jade fought a smile. "How come?"

"Because Mom's already talking about how I'm going to be their babysitter so they can keep going out and on vacations. And I know she's not kidding. And I'm scared she's going to use it as another reason to keep me away from you and Dad." A tear slipped down her cheek and she impatiently rubbed it away. "It's stupid and unfair. I didn't ask her to have a baby. I shouldn't have to take care of it."

Murky, mucky ground here. "No. Of course the baby shouldn't be your responsibility, but you can help some, right?"

"I guess." Olivia shrugged. "But I know Mom's not going to stop there. She and Steven go out three or four nights every week. They aren't going to want to change that. And they like to take vacations, too. They're not going to take the baby with them. They never take me."

Jade's heart broke—again—for Tommy's daughter. "Oh, honey. They can't leave you in charge of a baby while they're on vacation."

"Watch them."

Elise started to fuss.

Indigo reached for the baby and stood, bouncing her up and down. "Does your dad know?"

"I don't think so. I'm not supposed to say anything." Olivia's hand flew to her mouth. "Oh, man."

"Hey. It's okay. Generally, I don't think anything good comes of adults asking kids to keep secrets." Jade frowned. She understood why Mel didn't want Liv mentioning it, though. It was definitely information Don needed. The question became, did Jade tell Tommy or did she try to get Liv to do it? "Your dad and I both want you to always feel safe telling us stuff. Anything. Ever. No matter what."

"Even things that I'm pretty sure will make you stop loving me?"

"Not possible." Jade saw Indigo and the baby slip down the hall, leaving them with a little privacy. It was nice that Elise was spending the day with Betsy in town. As improved as Jade and Elise's relationship was, Olivia was unlikely to have opened up in front of the other woman. "Look at me."

Olivia looked up.

Jade held her gaze steady. "Your dad is never going to stop loving you. I am never going to stop loving you. Period."

Olivia sniffled. "Okay."

"Okay." She paused and glanced down at her knitting, then back up. "I think you should tell your dad about the new baby."

"But my mom—"

"He needs to know if he's going to be able to help you." Was it possible for something like this to get Tommy primary physical custody? Don was still working on the change of venue and hitting up against a reasonable amount of resistance. Whatever contacts Mel's parents had, they had long-reaching arms. Jade shouldn't mention it—no point in getting Liv's hopes up. But at thirteen, shouldn't Olivia's preferences be taken into consideration, too?

"There's no way for him to help." Olivia sighed. "I know how Mom is. And Gran and Gramps, for that matter, too. Just forget it."

"Tell your dad at least. Please?"

Olivia shrugged. "Maybe."

Should she push? No. Not yet. Maybe she could think up a way to let Tommy know there was something he should ask Liv about. At least it was only Monday, so they had a week to figure it out. Jade sent a quick prayer heavenward. Because if anyone could untangle this situation, it was going to have to be Jesus.

"That's looking really pretty, hon." Tommy sat beside Olivia and picked up the finished length of scarf that dripped off her knitting needles. "You've got a knack."

"Thanks, Dad." Pleasure shone from Olivia's eyes, though her cheeks pinked.

Jade smiled, watching Tommy interact with Liv. He was a good dad. Maybe even a great one. It would be fun to see him with a newborn.

That thought had been lingering in her mind since the conversation with Indigo on Monday. It didn't hurt, of course, that she and Tommy were continuing to get closer to one another in the evenings after Olivia went to bed. Babies were a natural extension of that, weren't they? Even if, right now, they were taking precautions, she couldn't help the occasional wistful thought.

But it wasn't a conversation to have now, while Liv was in town. It was better to wait—probably better to wait even longer, given the Mel situation. And seriously, what was it going to take to get Olivia to tell Tommy about the baby and Mel's expectations for her older daughter?

Tommy was a great dad, and he and Olivia had a surprisingly good relationship, given the wrenches Mel had tried to throw in that over the years, but apparently the girl couldn't quite break away from her mother's request for secrecy.

Should Jade?

"You've got three days left."

"It's really only two, Dad. I fly out on Sunday. If we go to church in the morning, we'll only have time to eat lunch and say goodbye to everyone before we have to start the drive to Albuquerque."

He nodded. "You're right."

Jade mentally pumped her fist. Church was something she and Tommy *had* talked about. They'd agreed not to push it, and see what happened. Maybe, just maybe, this was a prayer God was going to answer sooner rather than later.

"Do you think we'd have time to talk to your lawyer?"

Tommy's eyebrows lifted. "Don? Why? What's up?"

Olivia's gaze flicked over to Jade.

Jade shook her head slightly.

For the briefest moment, relief was visible on Olivia's face. She turned back to Tommy. "Mom's pregnant. She's said a few things about me babysitting all the time—I don't want to."

"Honey, I can't keep your mom from asking you to babysit. Plus, a little extra money's always good, right?" He frowned. "I get why you'd be upset about a baby after all these years, but—"

"No, Dad, you don't get it." Olivia threw down her knitting and lurched to her feet. "You tell him, Jade."

Jade's shoulders fell as Olivia fled the room. She sighed.

"What'd I miss? I thought teenage girls loved babies. Why isn't this good news?" Tommy raked his hand through his hair. "Just when I thought we were skimming past hormones."

"Tommy." Jade shook her head and reached for his hand. "Don't blindly attribute women's moods to hormones, okay? It makes you sound like a jerk."

He bristled. "Excuse me."

"Look. It's not paid babysitting here and there. At least not from what she said on Monday."

"Monday? You've known about this since Monday?" Tommy pushed to his feet and stalked across the room. "Why wouldn't you mention it?"

"Because Olivia didn't want me to. It's her news. I've been nudging her to share all week. Will you please sit down?" The man's irritated pacing was making Jade grumpy. This wasn't how the conversation was supposed to go at all.

"I expect you to tell me things about my daughter." Tommy flopped into a chair on the other side of the room.

It hurt. Jade squashed the feeling, but it lingered in the back of her mind despite her efforts. "It was clear she didn't want me to. I'm not going to betray her trust, Tommy."

His lips thinned. "Fine. Do go on."

She winced at the rancor in his voice. "I guess Mel has said —or implied, I didn't probe too deeply—"

He snorted.

"Do you mind? We're still learning our relationship, too."

Tommy waved a hand. She took it as permission to continue.

"As I was saying, Olivia believes Mel and Steven intend to continue to go out three and four nights a week, leaving her in charge of the baby. She also believes Mel plans to leave her in charge of the baby—ostensibly under the care of her grandparents, but you and I know how that has been so far—while they travel. She'd be like a nanny."

“Mel can’t do that.”

“She shouldn’t, no, but she can if no one stops her. Are Mel’s parents going to do something?” Surely grandparents would step in, wouldn’t they?

Tommy scrubbed his hands over his face. “I don’t know. They’re busy people, too. They like to go out—see and be seen at the club, that kind of thing. Best I can see them doing is hiring an actual nanny to watch both of them.”

That might not be too bad. Depending, of course, on the nanny. Would a nanny help with a teenager? Or would it just be assumed she was fine and all attention would be spent on the baby?

“She’s right. I need to talk to Don. I hate that. This is going to be a problem. Mel’s good at twisting what people say—what Olivia says. It hasn’t happened yet. I’m a little worried Don is going to say we have to wait until it does before we can act.” Tommy slammed a fist into his hand. “I hate having to be reactive like that.”

“You should go talk to her.” Olivia needed to see that her dad was torn up by this. She needed to know Tommy wanted to act—that he was going to try—that he took her seriously.

He blew out a breath. “Yeah. I’ll do that.”

Jade watched him stand and move toward the back of the cabin where the bedrooms were. He stopped at the doorway and turned. “I’m sorry for snapping.”

She managed a slight smile. “It’s okay.”

He shook his head and disappeared into the hallway. Jade listened as he knocked, then heard the quiet murmur of their voices before the door clicked shut.

She rubbed a hand over her heart. He’d apologized. Did she need to? She had kept information from him—but she’d told him before this that she wanted to start things off on the right foot with Olivia. That meant keeping her confidences.

Of course, in this situation, Liv hadn't explicitly asked Jade to keep quiet. It had seemed implied, but maybe Jade had been wrong.

This was hard. She'd known it would be—marriage and an instant family had to be an adjustment.

But it sure felt like she was failing.

16

Tommy slid the turquoise nugget set in silver up the cords of his bolo tie and studied his reflection in the mirror. He'd been getting a lot of mileage out of his suit lately. But even so, it was good he'd caved and rented a tux for his wedding to Jade. He smiled. They were coming up on ten weeks—nearly three months—and it was going well. At least, he thought so.

Jade knocked on the bathroom door. "You about ready?"

"Sure. Did you need something?" He stepped out and gestured for her to go in. "It's all yours."

"I'm nearly ready. It's nice not having to be there early because we're in the wedding. I'm glad Royal and Sophie kept their wedding party small." Jade leaned closer to the mirror and flicked mascara onto her eyelashes. She screwed it closed and reached for one of the several tubes of lipstick she kept lined up like soldiers on the vanity before flicking her gaze up and meeting his in the mirror. "Were you going to watch?"

"I can't admire my beautiful wife?"

Her cheeks darkened and she focused on applying her lipstick. "There. I'm set."

"You look amazing."

She did, too. The green dress hugged her curves in all the right places. His fingers itched to touch. To pull her closer and explore those curves. Except, of course, they'd end up missing her half-brother's wedding. And that would be hard to explain. Tommy settled for holding out his hand.

She took it and threaded her fingers through his. "I could say the same."

He held her gaze as his heart thundered in his ears. "We should go."

"We really should." Jade's gaze flicked to their bed and her cheeks pinked again. "Come on. We didn't have to be early, but we shouldn't be late."

Tommy let her lead him from the bedroom, through the cabin, and out to the truck. He opened her door and helped her in before moving around to the driver's side and climbing up. "Have you heard from Olivia?"

Jade shook her head. "Not this week. Actually, not since last Wednesday."

He nodded. The Wednesday after she'd gotten home from her week with them was the last time he'd heard from her as well. It was only a week and a half, but it was a change. Change, when Mel was involved, always made him suspicious. "I wish she could've come down for this. Seems my girl likes weddings."

"It does, doesn't it?" Jade sighed. "That would've been nice. I don't think there was ever any chance, though."

"I know. It grates on me. And I'm worried about why she hasn't at least texted you." He didn't have to love the fact that his daughter was more likely to reach out to Jade, but he could accept it. Woman-to-woman talks, he'd been informed, were an important part of growing up. "Maybe we should give her a call after the reception."

"Absolutely. And I'll go one better than that. When we get to the church, let's take a selfie and I'll text it to her and let her know to expect our call. Maybe priming the pump, so to speak, is a better plan."

He smiled. "Sounds good. I won't mind recording how good you look."

Jade laughed.

The drive into town was quiet. He turned the radio on, and they both made little forays into conversation, but it fizzled out. That was normal, right? Just because a couple was married didn't mean they always had tons to say to one another. It didn't mean something was wrong.

"Do you consider Royal your brother?"

"Half-brother."

Tommy's eyebrows lifted. "That's fast."

"Sorry. It's knee-jerk. It's a good question. I don't know. I haven't really thought about it. And of all of them, I've really only gotten close with Skye and Indigo. Royal and I had a rocky start. That's mostly my fault. Or all my fault. I should probably apologize to him, to be honest." Jade sighed. "I know that rough start has kept me from seeking out time with just him and Sophie. I'm embarrassed."

"Why? What happened?"

"Ugh. I was in a bad place—well, that kind of defines a lot of my life up until maybe a year ago. Anyway, Royal and Sophie were in Phoenix and I arranged to be out there to meet a client, which I could have done virtually, but I was trying to pin down my dad. They met me at a restaurant and I was just awful. About everything." Jade turned and stared out the window, her head shaking slightly.

"Hey. I know everyone at the ranch—Royal and Sophie included—love you now." Heat crawled up his neck. He was including himself in that, but it was true. Maybe she wouldn't notice. It wasn't as if he'd come out with a declaration. On the other hand, surely she knew. She had to, didn't she?

She turned back to look at him. "They do?"

He nodded as he pulled into the church parking lot.

A smile played at the corners of her lips. "That's handy. I love everyone at the ranch, too."

A tightness around his heart he hadn't realized was there eased. He pulled into a parking spot and cut the engine. "You ready?"

"I am. Weddings are fun." Jade pushed her door open and got out of the truck.

Fun? That wasn't a word he'd use. His suit was comfortable enough, but it wasn't like he was volunteering to wear it every day. Or even every Sunday. The fact that most of the churches he'd attended were happy to have you through the doors, regardless of attire, was a seriously good thing in his mind. Maybe the people who harped on attire as a show of reverence had a point—he could give them that—but he'd still choose come-as-you-are over fancy Sunday duds any day.

Tommy hopped down from the truck and glanced over at Jade.

On the other hand. Seeing his wife—and wow, he loved being able to use that word, if only to himself—dressed up? That was something he was going to try to arrange more often.

Even if it also put him back in the suit.

"Did I mention you look pretty?"

Jade smiled and reached for his hand. "You did, but I never mind hearing it."

Tommy leaned close and brushed his lips over hers. He paused and shifted back, giving her a longer, lingering kiss.

"Hey, you two."

Tommy eased away and cleared his throat. He scanned the

parking lot and saw Indigo and Joaquin getting out of their truck, laughing. He lifted a hand. "Hey."

Jade fell into step beside him, her hand still in his. They caught up with Indigo and Joaquin and the four of them headed into the church.

Tommy looked around the foyer. It was similar to the church he attended—probably most churches were—although this one had some trendier looking signs directing people toward various locations. It was probably good for visitors. The church the Hewitts attended was bigger than the one he and Joaquin had chosen. Not by a lot. But probably enough that letting visitors know where the welcome center was turned out to be a good thing.

"They have a welcome center?" Joaquin shook his head. "We have Miss Ethel."

Tommy chuckled. "She's better than any welcome center could be."

Jade nodded. "That woman's amazing. She knew my name before I even realized I was going to stick around."

"That's Miss Ethel." Indigo grinned. "She adores baby Elise."

"Speaking of baby Elise, where is she?" Jade frowned.

Tommy hadn't even noticed they were there without the baby carrier—or the baby.

"We left her with a babysitter. We've been talking to the youth pastor to see if he had recommendations of mature, responsible teenagers to babysit. Figured this was a good trial run since they're having the reception back at the camp lodge like Skye and Morgan did. We can head back or just go get her if the sitter's having trouble." Indigo shrugged. "I won't lie and say I'm not nervous, but Maria has been pushing us to get it figured out for a while. I guess she and Cyan have someone they use every couple of weeks so they still get date time."

Tommy nodded. He and Mel had done many date nights—

she'd been adamant. For whatever reason, it hadn't been the magic fix that the Internet seemed to suggest it would be, but whatever. It wasn't as if he didn't see the need for couples to spend time together connecting without their children. It was more that date night wasn't the bandage that was going to fix brokenness. That could only happen when both parties were willing to be honest about their own flaws and commit to working on them—separately and together.

Jade glanced over. "Do we go on dates enough for you?"

"I think we're okay. Sometimes just being together at the end of the day and spending time alone is the same thing. Why?" Was she worried? Was he letting her down already? "Did you want to go out? We could plan a trip to Santa Fe."

"Not unless you want to. I like being with you at home, too." Jade leaned closer.

Indigo and Joaquin exchanged a knowing look.

"What's the look for?" Jade frowned.

"You don't have kids. Or not full time. It's different. Not saying you won't feel the same way when you do, but keep an open mind." Indigo reached over and patted Jade's arm. "For us, this is a good testing ground and we'll see how it goes."

Jade nodded.

It was true. He and Jade didn't have kids. They were more traditional newlyweds compared to Indigo and Joaquin. Especially compared to them, seeing as how they'd made a baby before they were even dating. But they'd worked it out, or maybe it was more honest to say God had worked it out. He'd done amazing things in both of their lives and the end result had been a wedding on the same day Indigo went into labor.

They followed the usher down the aisle and took their seats behind Betsy, Wayne, and Elise Hewitt. The sanctuary was filling up. It wasn't a huge surprise. From things Sophie had said here and there when she'd been at one of the lunches at the ranch, her mom had invited anyone with even a slim connection to the family. Apparently, that was important to her, and Sophie had been willing to indulge her mother.

His lips twitched. She probably would have been seriously displeased with his wedding to Jade if either of them had been her child.

Before long, Royal and Sophie stood, hands clasped, in front of the pastor. The way the two of them looked at each other, it was clear they loved. Deeply.

A tiny twinge of something he couldn't name hit Tommy in his heart. Had anyone ever looked at him like that? Mel hadn't at their wedding. Jade certainly hadn't. It was okay. It wouldn't matter.

They had a marriage and it was already helping things along with Mel and getting to see Olivia. He warmed. Having his daughter here for the whole of spring break had been amazing. Why hadn't she called since, though? Or texted. Even before, when Mel kept her away, he'd gotten a text or call every week.

Jade bumped him with her elbow and sent him a questioning look.

He shook his head, clearing the worried thoughts out of the way. He focused back on the ceremony as Royal and Sophie lit an intricately carved candle with individual tapers. The unity candle. Another thing he hadn't had at either of his weddings. Mel hadn't wanted any of what she termed the religious trappings—he hadn't argued. It wasn't as if he'd been a believer at the time. With Jade he would have liked it. If they'd been getting married after a friendship and courtship like most relationships.

His stomach sank. Had they been wrong to do this?

He kept his attention fixed on the ceremony, but his gaze darted to Jade.

He didn't hear the rest of the wedding. He went through the motions, clapping when the new couple was presented as husband and wife. He smiled as they passed by and again in the receiving line.

In the truck, Jade fastened her seatbelt and stared at him. "You okay?"

"Yeah. Sorry. Of course, I am." He offered a smile. "It was a beautiful wedding."

"Was it?" Jade smiled. "I didn't get the impression that you actually saw much of it."

He searched back through the afternoon. Had his mind wandered that much? He shrugged. "It was a wedding. It seemed nice."

Jade laughed. "It was. Are you sure you're all right? Are you worried about Olivia?"

He nodded. That was definitely part of it.

"Why don't we give her a call? Maybe she'll pick up this time." Jade took her cell out of her purse and tapped the screen. "I put it on speaker."

The sound of ringing filled the truck's cab as they headed back up toward the ranch for the reception. When Olivia's voice started the recorded greeting, Jade started to end the call.

"No. Wait. Let's leave a message."

Jade nodded. At the beep, she spoke. "Hey Livy. It's Jade and your dad."

"Hi, honey."

"We're starting to get a little worried about you. Can you please just shoot me or your dad a text, or give us a call, and let us know you're okay? Love you."

"I love you, Livy. Looking forward to you coming for the summer." Tommy tried to keep his voice upbeat and full of cheer.

"Bye, hon." Jade ended the call and bit her lip. "Should you call Mel?"

He'd been debating the same thing. "I don't know. It's been

so nice not to have to deal with her. I guess maybe I'll text Don and see what he thinks."

She nodded. "I hate that something like this has to go through him."

"I know. But I seem to make it worse when I talk to her. If Liv's doing fine and just busy, I don't want to give Mel a reason to make her life hard."

"Okay. I'll keep praying."

"Me, too." He reached over for Jade's hand, and the warmth of her touch soothed all of the aches in his soul. Maybe they hadn't had a traditional wedding. Maybe things with Mel were always ugly and complicated. And maybe he was worried about his daughter. But it was going to be okay. He just needed to remember the reason he'd gotten married in the first place. Olivia.

Everything he could do for his daughter, he was going to do.

Now, he'd push it all out of his mind and enjoy an evening of good food and fellowship with friends as they celebrated Royal and Sophie's marriage.

Tomorrow would be soon enough to worry again.

17

Jade clicked End on the call with the woman who was rapidly becoming her favorite author to work for, and leaned back in her chair, stretching her arms over her head. It was definitely time to get up and move around a little. This author had teamed up with ten others and was putting together a big Mother's Day promotion. Nothing like waiting until the last minute, since that was this coming Sunday. At least she'd gotten in touch today so Jade had the full work week ahead of her to get stuff done. But there were going to be some long days in there since she did have other work scheduled already, too.

Still. This author was always polite and friendly. And she'd added a tip to a couple of the invoices Jade had sent when things had been more time consuming than either of them originally thought. So she'd make it work.

Her phone lit up with a text notification and Jade grabbed at it, praying it would be Olivia. It had been almost a full month since either she or Tommy'd had any contact with the girl. Don was on it, but he was running into roadblocks left and right.

They'd gotten assurances from Mel to Mel's lawyer to Don to them that Olivia was fine, but it didn't ease either of their minds.

If anything, it made them both more suspicious.

Mel said she'd taken Olivia's phone away as punishment. But for a month? And she wouldn't tell them what Liv was supposed to have done to warrant it, either. It was all such a mess.

Jade tapped to open her texts and blinked back tears. Not Olivia. And she didn't need a coupon for BOGO froyo right now.

She set a timer on her phone, stood, and tucked the phone into her pocket. She'd go for a quick walk to get the blood moving again and then she needed to reach out to her contacts at some of the book promo email lists and also start on graphics. Maybe she should take a couple of minutes and make a prioritized list, too.

Walking through the living room, she looked around. It was still strange that she lived in this cabin with Tommy. They were coming up on three months. It had to start feeling real soon, didn't it? Of course, being out of touch with Olivia—the whole reason behind their marriage—wasn't helping anything.

Tommy was worried. Jade understood, because she was worried, too. But he frequently snapped at her. And no matter how quick he was to apologize, it didn't ease the tension in her chest or soothe away the fear that their marriage was going to be over before it really had a chance to start. If Mel removed Olivia from Tommy's life—if the courts allowed it—he wouldn't need Jade anymore. Would he want her?

She blew out a breath and stepped onto the porch. She breathed in the clean, mountain air. Indigo's sheep were bleating in the distance. Maybe she'd walk over that way and watch them and the alpacas. There were babies this year in the sheep pens and Indigo was talking about breeding a couple of the alpacas in the summer. That would be interesting.

Everyone was busy with whatever kept them occupied, so while there were signs of industry, she didn't see anyone out and about. Tommy had said something about the camp this morning at breakfast. Jade hadn't listened—she'd been trying to keep her head down and not bring up Olivia.

Starting the day with a disagreement was getting old.

She frowned. So much for keeping her mind off that problem. She shook her head and focused on breathing in and out.

"Out for a walk?" Indigo had a foot up on the rail of the alpaca pen.

"Yeah. Needed to clear my head."

"Must be the day for it. Elise shooed me out of the shop."

Jade cocked her head to the side. "What happened?"

Indigo's lips thinned. "Why did something have to happen?"

"Because that doesn't sound like Elise. And baby Elise isn't with you either, so I'm guessing you left in a hurry."

Indigo sighed and crossed her arms on the top rail. "We had a couple of walk-ins. We're getting more of that now that the weather is better. They were touching everything—"

"Are you not supposed to touch the yarn?" Jade always reached out to rub two or three different colors between her fingers when she went to the fiber cabin.

"No, it's fine. I get that people want to know how soft it is. But it wasn't as if they were looking at the colors, commenting on it, and then reaching out. It was more like it was a free-for-all of touching. They were like toddlers at the children's museum."

Jade chuckled. Okay, that could be annoying.

"Then they started pulling things off the hooks and rubbing them on their cheeks and I guess one of them caught sight of a price tag, made a snotty comment about how high it was, and I might have snapped." Indigo shook her head. "I know better. I do. But you'd think they would, too. We're very clear on the website and anywhere we advertise that all the yarn is handmade from the animal up. Don't people recognize that means it's going to cost a bit more than the polyester junk imported from China?"

"They should." Jade had run into a few authors who had been less than diplomatic about expressing their sticker shock for her services. It was fine. She didn't want to be the lowest bidder. She had enough work, and she knew the value of her time. She'd seen in one author group where she'd been labeled "arrogant" because of it—oh, they hadn't used her name, but it had been obvious to Jade—but whatever. "I'm sorry. Your yarn is lovely. And soft. And worth every penny because not only do you make it all by hand, you do it with love. I have to believe anything made with your yarn is going to be better because of that."

Indigo turned and smiled. "Thank you. I shouldn't let it get to me. It's not all their fault. I found out this morning I'm not pregnant, and I really thought I was. And I guess I hadn't realized how much I wanted to be until right then."

Jade nodded.

"It's stupid. Elise isn't even a year old yet. It's too soon, probably, but I'm ready. We're ready. And it was easy—and accidental—the first time. I don't understand why it's taking longer now that we want it. So I came out to see the alpacas. They don't get pregnant easily, either."

"They don't?" Jade mimicked Indigo's pose on the fence and watched the funny looking animals. She hadn't spent any time—ever—pondering the intricacies of animal husbandry. Wasn't the process pretty simple?

"No. The females only ovulate during mating. So there's no guarantee. You have to get them together, see if they can figure out the act—which implies a lot of willingness on her part or the male is going to get injured. If they do, then you have to wait and try again. If she lets him, then she didn't get pregnant the first time. They gestate for about a year, so you have to time it based on when you want them to deliver—when it's best for the cria, the baby. It's complicated." Indigo shrugged. "I guess it's not all that different from people."

Jade snorted. "People are definitely complicated."

Indigo looked over. "Trouble in paradise?"

Jade looked away.

"Sorry. I'm so sorry. This is why Elise suggested the walk. That was snippy and mean and I'm sorry."

Jade's lips twitched. "Maybe if you said you were sorry, I would forgive you."

Indigo laughed. "Sorry. And thanks. Do you want to share?"

"I don't know." Jade brushed hair out of her eyes and tucked it behind her ear. "This thing with Olivia is stressing Tommy out. And me. And it all sort of snowballs, you know?"

"Still nothing? That's frustrating. I wonder if your mom felt that way?"

"What do you mean?"

"Or maybe in reverse? Did she wish Dad was in touch with you? That he wanted to hear from you and see you? Did it make her life harder because he was so rigid about cutting her off?"

She hadn't even thought about her mom with this latest development. Would Mom have wanted her to know Martin Hewitt? Probably not. The conversations they'd had about him had never been positive. Mostly because Martin had made it clear from day one that there wasn't a future where the two of them were married, and that had always been Mom's goal.

"I don't know. I can't blame either of them, really. They both made horrible choices and then paid the consequences. At this point, I guess I'm happy to leave it all in the past. They're both gone anyway, so it's not like I can talk to them about it. There's no happy ending here."

"Isn't there?" Indigo gestured to the ranch. "You're here. You're connected to the Hewitts. And you've found love. That seems like a happy ending."

"You're right." Jade forced a smile. She hadn't found love, but she didn't need to argue with Indigo about it. She didn't even want to argue with herself about it. She'd thought—hoped—that when their relationship had shifted to include more physical intimacy, it was the beginning of that deeper emotional connection. And it had been that way. At first. But now? It didn't seem like she'd accomplished her goal to make a place for herself at the ranch.

Marrying Tommy was supposed to prove her usefulness. Not leave her heartbroken.

"Hi, honey, I'm home!" Tommy's voice rang out with a definite *I Love Lucy* inflection to it.

Jade smiled and checked the time. It was later than she'd realized—she'd meant to start dinner. She saved her work then shut down her laptop. Maybe she could talk Tommy into heading down to the Cantina. They weren't super busy on Mondays, and not cooking sounded like just the thing.

She turned off the light in Olivia's room—she couldn't call it her office anymore, not when she so desperately wished her stepdaughter would get in touch—and headed to the living room.

"There's my gorgeous wife." He crossed the room and swept her into his arms before dipping her back and lowering his mouth to hers.

"Well, hi there." She clung to his shoulders and gave in to the sensations that zipped through her. "You had a good day, I guess?"

Tommy righted her, still holding her close. "I did. We marked out the area where the mission camp obstacle course is going to go."

"Already? It's barely May. Aren't they coming in August?"

"Yeah, but it'll take some time to build and it's one that we've decided to make permanent. It'll be a draw for youth groups, if no one else. The plans are pretty cool. Did you see them?"

She'd been at the main house when Wayne was talking them over with Tommy and Joaquin, but she hadn't paid attention. All her focus had been on the scarf she was trying to finish knitting so she'd have it to show Olivia the next time they did a video call. She shook her head.

"Ah. I have them, if you want to see?"

"Sure." She leaned up, unable to resist brushing her lips over his one more time. "How do you feel about tacos?"

"I love tacos."

"How do you feel about the Cantina?"

He laughed. "I see where this is going. Let me grab a shower and then I'm game. Monday night date night should be a thing."

That had been easier than expected. Was his whole system on alert like hers was? Could she have been wrong this afternoon? "Maybe it should."

Before too long, Tommy had showered and they made their way down the hill to town. Parking was easy and they were seated quickly.

Tommy reached across the table and took her hand. "This is nice. It was a good idea. Thanks for thinking of it."

Her cheeks warmed. She just hadn't wanted to cook. Or to go to dinner at the main house with Betsy and Wayne, who inevitably saw too much, no matter how she tried to hide it. "Thanks for agreeing."

"Do you know what you're getting?" Tommy kept one hand on the menu and held her gaze.

Jade picked up her menu and hid behind it while she studied the offerings. She probably didn't need to look—she loved their tamales stuffed with pork and green chile—but she also didn't want to meet his eyes. "Maybe? What about you?"

"Tacos."

She set the menu down and looked at him. "Really?"

"You put the idea in my head. I couldn't shake it loose." Tommy shrugged. "They're good here."

A young woman wearing the Cantina uniform approached their table with a heaping bowl of tortilla chips and a smaller bowl of salsa so hot Jade could almost feel it scorching her tongue already. She set the chips and salsa down. "Hi. Can I get your drink orders?"

"Jade?"

"Just water, please."

"I'll have a lemonade. I think we're ready to order." Tommy glanced over at Jade.

She nodded. Why pretend she was getting anything else? "I'll have the tamales, please. Just rice on the side, no beans."

"The tacos." Tommy tapped his menu. "Thanks."

"Sure." The girl disappeared with a smile.

Jade reached for a chip and dunked it in the salsa. Just like she thought, it was spicy and amazing as it hit her tongue. She closed her eyes. "Mmm."

Tommy crunched a chip and nodded. "Exactly. How was your day?"

"Okay, I guess." She filled him in on the big project she'd taken on in the morning and a little of her conversation with Indigo. At least the part about Indigo snapping at her clients. Jade wasn't going to share her insecurities about their marriage, nor was she going to be the one to mention Olivia. This had been a pleasant evening so far, and she'd like to keep it that way.

"They're already trying for another? That's . . ." He shook his head, but his gaze stayed locked on her. "It seems too soon. They haven't even been married a year."

"And baby Elise isn't a year old yet either." Jade reached for a chip, desperate to keep her hands busy. Why was he looking at her so intently? Did she want kids? Yes, absolutely. And at the start of all this, they'd agreed that they'd get there. But the way things were going now, was that realistic?

"Well, good for them, I guess. It's interesting about the alpacas."

She laughed. "You would think so. I thought it was little TMI and felt bad for the girls. They were standing right there, minding their own business, and she's giving away all the secrets and struggles."

"You know they're not people, right? They're animals and they don't understand English?"

"Yes." Jade stuck out her tongue. "And yet."

He smiled.

The server came back with their drinks and refilled the chips. "Your food should be up soon."

Tommy waited as the server walked away. "Don called me today."

Jade raised her eyebrows. "Oh?"

"I guess Mel's attorneys have now stopped returning his calls. Which suggests that there's something bad going on up there and Mel is circling the wagons."

Her stomach sank. "What are we going to do?"

"I'm going to drive up this weekend and see if I can get her to talk to me. Or at least see Livy. Maybe take her a cell phone that's just for contacting us. Don was thinking a pre-paid phone without any bells and whistles—something that makes it clear all she's doing is calling or texting us—would be a good compromise." He shrugged. "I don't think Mel will go for it, but I'll give it a shot."

He was driving up. He didn't even invite her? Or ask if she wanted to come? Should she ask? Except what if he said no? Which one would be the right choice—and make it clear she was invested in Olivia too, without opening her heart up for more pain? "Why don't you think Mel will go for it?"

"Because she's Mel." He blew out a breath and waited while a different server put plates in front of them and scooted away. Tommy reached for Jade's hand. "Can we pray?"

"Of course." She squeezed his fingers and bowed her head.

Tommy said a quick prayer of thanks for the food, asking for wisdom in how to deal with Mel and Olivia as well. "Amen."

"Amen. So, Mel?"

"She's not big on compromise. I learned that when we were dating. I thought it was funny, at first. Then, once we were married, I realized how hard it was to live with someone who had to always be right and in control." He picked up a taco and crunched in.

"She really is a younger version of my mom. I'm sorry." Jade peeled the corn husk away from her tamale and breathed in the rich scent of corn, tomatoes, pork, and chile. Her mouth watered. She glanced up and studied Tommy before taking a deep breath and asking, "Can I come?"

"Come?" He shot her a quizzical look before he figured it out. "To Colorado?"

"I'm worried about Liv, too. And maybe I could be, I don't know, some sort of buffer?"

Tommy snorted and shook his head. "I don't think that's a good idea. Mel's not going to want to see me. She's sure not going to let you anywhere near Liv."

She'd known better than to ask, but even still, it sliced

though her heart. It was a wonder there wasn't blood visibly seeping through her shirt. Jade cut into the tamale and took a bite. It might as well have been sawdust. But she wasn't going to let him know that. He already had too much power, because he mattered too much. "If you change your mind, let me know."

18

Tommy parked his truck at the curb in front of Mel's parents' mansion. He'd only been there two times before. Neither one had gone over particularly well. Mel was largely at fault for both of them, although he was a big enough man to understand he'd played along. Her parents had hated him from day one. To them, he was one step up from homeless. He didn't have a degree—and they didn't care that Mel didn't either, standards weren't meant to be applied evenly across the board. Even before Hope Ranch, he'd taken jobs that most people considered menial. Handyman work. Ranch work. Stable work.

He liked to be outside and for his duties to vary. A nine-to-five in an office? He shuddered. That wasn't the life for him.

And sitting here wasn't helping him see that Olivia was all right.

Tommy pushed open the door and climbed down, his muscles groaning in relief after the long drive. Steeling himself, he strode up the walkway to the front door and pressed the bell.

It was a long wait. They were watching him, he was sure. Their doorbell camera was obvious, as were the cameras on either end of the porch. Did they expect him to just walk away if they didn't come?

Tommy gave them five minutes, then pressed the doorbell again. He could do this all day, if that was what needed to happen.

Hoping his face reflected his determination, he gazed directly into the camera above the doorbell and allowed the corners of his mouth to lift into a sardonic smile.

Footsteps approached the door and then, finally, it was opened.

Mel crossed her arms and stood in the doorway. "Go away, Tommy."

"I'd like to see my daughter, Mel."

"I told you she was fine. And it's not your weekend. It's Mother's Day tomorrow—pretty sure that means me. Not you or the whore you convinced to marry you. Like my lawyers didn't see right through that."

Fire burned in his gut and he clenched his jaw. His words came out from between his teeth. "Jade is not a whore. I'll ask you to leave my wife out of this and go get Olivia. I'd like five minutes with her and then I'll go."

"No."

He waited. A short answer wasn't Mel's style. The silence stretched. Then snapped as he knew it would.

Mel frowned. "She isn't here right now, anyway. Steven took her out to get me a gift."

Tommy nodded. "I'll wait."

"Go away, Tommy. She's fine."

"No." Unlike Mel, he was perfectly content to leave it there. He shifted to study the porch before settling on the front step.

Mel's breath hissed out. "You can't sit there."

"It's a nice day. This way, Liv should see me when they get

back. Five minutes, Mel. I'm serious." Tommy stretched his legs out and looked around the neighborhood.

"I'm going to call the cops."

"Good idea. I've got information about our custody arrangement, which includes unrestricted conversations with whichever parent isn't currently hosting her." He patted his pocket. "It'd be great to have them go ahead and enforce that."

"Oh, please. You forget where you are? The cops I call aren't going to care about your paperwork."

"I have the number for the state police right here as well. Maybe I'll call and explain the situation to them. I heard your father's having a little trouble right now with some of his state-level friends." That had been good news when Don had unearthed it. Mel's father had brokered a land deal with some of the bigwigs in Colorado government. The deal had gone south, money was missing and, at least in the larger arena, her daddy was persona non grata.

Mel paled. "They don't have jurisdiction here."

He simply smiled. Technically she wasn't wrong, but they both knew with the way things were right now for her father, the state police were motivated to find a way to have a longer conversation with the man. "Five minutes with Olivia, then I'll go."

"I hate you."

"I know." It pained him. He didn't love her anymore, if he ever had, but she was the mother of his daughter. At one time, they'd had something together and he still grieved for its loss. If only for Olivia's sake.

"Fine. But when she gets here, I'm setting a timer. Not a minute more."

He nodded. He didn't expect anything less. It was enough that she'd caved.

"Don't expect to use the bathroom or get a drink. I don't know how long they'll be gone, and I'm not calling Steven."

"That's fine. Like I said, it's a beautiful day."

The door slammed shut, the bullet-like report bouncing off the house across the street.

Tommy slid his phone out of his pocket and texted Jade and then Don to let them know how things were going. Then he pulled up an online Sudoku game and settled in to wait.

IT WAS JUST GOING to dusk when headlights turned up the driveway.

Tommy stood and stretched, working the kinks out. The drive up and then several hours of sitting on concrete were hard on a guy.

"Daddy!" The car door slammed shut and Olivia raced to him. She threw her arms around his middle and squeezed. Then she burst into tears.

"Get in the house, Olivia."

Tommy curved an arm around Olivia's shoulders and sent the man a long, cool stare. "You must be Steven. Why don't you go inside and find Mel? She'll explain."

Steven glared but stomped past them into the house.

When the door shut, Tommy hugged Liv tightly. "I only have five minutes. It's all I could get her to agree to. And you know she's timing."

Olivia grunted. "I'm sorry I got my phone taken away."

"Me, too. That's part of why I'm here." He eased away and took the cheap, disposable phone he'd bought her out of another pocket. "I was going to try and get your mom to agree to this, but I don't see that happening. So keep it out of sight. You only use this to text or call me and Jade though. Promise me."

"I promise. I don't have anyone else I want to talk to, anyway."

Tommy looked down at his daughter's tear-streaked face and frowned. "Can you tell me what's wrong?"

She shook her head.

"Are you safe?" His mind was conjuring up all sorts of terrible scenarios. All of them made him want to grab Olivia, toss her in the car, and take off. But the saner part of him knew that would cause more problems than it would solve.

She slid the phone into her purse and wiped her eyes. "It's not like that. People at school are being mean, and Mom says I just have to deal with it. I just wish—Dad, why are boys jerks?"

He winced. Teenage boys could definitely be jerks. He pulled her into another tight hug. "They don't know how to use their words, mostly. I'm sorry, sweetie. They get better once their hormones settle down."

Olivia sighed. "Is that like saying 'boys will be boys'?"

Was it? He'd never liked that phrase—as if it excused any sort of behavior. "I guess it is. I'm sorry. I'm not trying to excuse them. What are they doing? Are they teasing you?"

She shrugged one shoulder and her cheeks flamed red.

"Livy?"

She shook her head. "I don't wanna talk about it."

Should he push? "Is your mom handling it?"

"I guess."

That wasn't encouraging. Or definitive. He was so out of his depth. He'd been a teenage boy. He knew the sorts of things they did—or at least the sorts of things teenagers twenty years ago had done. But today was a whole new world with everything online. Online. Her phone. "Were they being mean online? Is that why your mom took away your phone?"

Olivia nodded slowly.

In that case, was giving her another phone a terrible idea? No. This one couldn't get on the Internet. He'd made sure of that. "Don't give out that new number to anyone."

"I won't. I don't even want the other phone back. Social media is stupid."

What had happened? Obviously some sort of bullying. But what? "Your mom hasn't given me details, hon, so I don't know how to help you."

"You can't." Her voice was a whisper. "I wish I could live with you full time."

"I'd love that." Don had told Tommy that at thirteen, most courts would take Olivia's wishes into consideration. The problem, of course, was that right now their case wasn't in "most courts." Although, the new information with the police might mean the court situation was changing, too. "Have you mentioned it to your mom?"

"And get murdered in my sleep? No, Dad, I'm not stupid."

His lips twitched. "I'm pretty sure she wouldn't murder you, but she'd definitely be upset."

"Especially since she's still banking on me babysitting all the time." Olivia sighed like the weight of the world rested solely on her shoulders.

Tommy tugged her close again and held her. What could he do? What was he supposed to do? "I'll talk to Don and let him know that's what you want. Maybe he can figure out a way to get your mom to agree."

Tears brimmed in Olivia's eyes, but also the tiniest flicker of hope. "Thanks."

"I can't promise."

"I know. I'm just glad you'll try. I love you, Dad."

"I love you, too, Liv." He brushed his lips across the top of his daughter's head as the front door swung in, and Mel glowered at him from the doorway.

"That's five minutes. Inside, Olivia."

Head hanging, shoulders slumped, Olivia trudged up the

steps and into the house. She paused on the doorstep to glance over her shoulder and offer a weak smile.

Why did it feel like he'd just sent her to the gallows? "Thank you, Mel, for giving me some time."

"She's fine. Like I said."

"I'd like to know what happened with the boys at school."

"Oh, please. Is she still whining about that? She's fine. It was no big deal."

"It was to her." How could Mel not see that? Or care? "And it was big enough you took her phone away."

"That's because she decided to try to get even." Mel crossed her arms and jutted out her chin. "They were threatening to suspend her."

"And the boys?" His blood was starting to boil. Surely Mel had seen to it that the boys were punished for whatever they'd done. Because Olivia wasn't one who took matters into her own hands unless she'd felt there were no other choices.

Mel waved that away. "They were having harmless fun, and she blew it out of proportion."

"I'd like the details."

"There's no point. It's handled. You can go now."

Tommy gritted his teeth. Don had reminded him to avoid engaging in any unnecessary arguments. This didn't feel like it was unnecessary, but it was probably unwinnable, which amounted to the same thing. He bit back what he wanted to say and fought for a friendly tone. "I hear congratulations are in order."

Mel narrowed her gaze. "What do you mean?"

Tommy glanced down at her subtly rounding belly. "Another baby? Congratulations to you and Steven."

Mel snorted. "Whatever."

Well, he'd tried to be civil. He nodded once and started back down the path to his truck. He'd go find some food and give Don a call. Then he could figure out if he was going to get a hotel for the night or head at least part of the way home.

Tomorrow was Mother's Day. That had slipped his mind when he'd decided to race up here. Was Jade expecting a gift? She wasn't, technically, a mother. But she'd become a stepmother the moment she married him. It was probably worth trying to get home in time to give her a card. Maybe some flowers.

He hadn't done either of those things in the time they'd been married.

He'd never remembered stuff like this with Mel, either. She'd thrown it in his face often enough.

He was messing this up left and right, wasn't he? It was why he should've known better than to believe he'd ever find someone and settle down again. How had Jade ever convinced him to give this a try?

He was just no good at it.

19

Jade clicked Send on the invoice and shot her hands in the air. "Yes!"

Chuckling, she looked over her shoulder and the heat in her cheeks faded. No one had seen her little display. Not that it was wrong to be excited about finishing a big project—successfully—and having a client who kept repeating how elated they were. It wasn't. But Tommy had been surly since he got back from Colorado on Sunday, and Jade was doing her best not to poke the bear.

She checked the time. Almost lunch. She'd head down to the main house and eat with the crew. Tommy had packed a sandwich without any explanation. Maybe he and Joaquin were going to be hanging out at the lodge and pushing hard on the obstacle course. The hurry still didn't make sense to Jade. They had two months plus a little before the missionary came. At this point, though, extra space from Tommy wasn't a bad thing.

Jade rubbed her hand over her heart. It shouldn't hurt. They hadn't gotten married with stars in their eyes. It had been an arrangement for Olivia's benefit. And for Tommy's benefit. He'd asked her, then, what she got out of it. Her answer hadn't been a lie. It just wasn't working out—she wasn't helping him. She wasn't helping Olivia. And she hadn't made any difference in how Betsy and Wayne treated and welcomed her as part of the ranch.

If she'd fallen in love with Tommy, that was her own problem. She certainly wasn't going to bother him with it.

She pushed the thoughts away and stood. Another couple of weeks and Olivia should be arriving for the summer. Then Jade would move her office out into the living room. She walked out of the bedroom, down the short hall, and eyed the space. There was a corner near the window that would work. She might need a desk of her own—teenage girls needed desk space, too.

She'd ask Betsy about it at lunch.

Jade crossed the living room and opened the front door. She laughed. It was raining. She'd been so lost in her own little world that she hadn't heard it. She stepped back into the cabin and slipped on her rain jacket. Flipping up the hood, she headed out—easing into a jog when the rain picked up. The droplets were falling with enough force they almost hurt.

She reached the mudroom door and tugged it open, running into a broad back when she rushed in.

"Whoa, there, tiger." Royal chuckled as he stepped forward.

"Sorry. Just trying to get out of the deluge." Jade scooted around her half-brother and toed off her shoes, nudging them closer to the pile that had grown beside the bench the Hewitts kept for that purpose. She shrugged out of her jacket and hung it on a peg. "How's your day?"

"Pretty good. Sophie has a couple of students who wanted an extra hour, so I'll grab her a plate for later, but I'm ready for a break. I feel like I'm hearing the rain in the background of the recordings, so I don't want to do more in case I end up having rerecord everything."

"Ugh. I hope you don't. Oh, hey, I gave your name to a couple of the authors I'm a virtual assistant for. If they reach out, they're supposed to mention my name."

"Thanks. I'll take any business I can get."

She glanced over. He didn't look worried. "Things slowing down?"

"Nah. We're good. It's just always nice to have work in the pipe, you know?"

She did know, now. Freelancing had never been something she'd planned on. Jade had always considered herself a nine-to-five office girl. She liked being on her own more than she'd anticipated. "Any idea what Maria made for lunch?"

Royal laughed. "Nope. Smells good, though. Why don't we go see?"

Jade followed him through the kitchen, taking care to stay out of Maria's way as she flipped sandwiches and ladled soup. Was it grilled cheese? That was perfect for the weather. Jade found a seat beside Betsy.

"Hi, honey. It feels like I haven't seen you all week."

Jade smiled at her grandmother. "You haven't. Big project—so I've been working through lunch."

"That's not good. You need breaks to keep your brain active." Elise sat on the other side of Betsy and frowned slightly. "If I'd known that, I would have come and dragged you away."

"She would, too." Indigo laughed from the other side of the counter, where she'd set up a high chair for the baby. "We close for lunch every day now."

"It's not like it impacts business." Elise sent Indigo a quelling look.

"No, you're right. The online orders still come in and I think we're just too far out of town to ever be a going concern for walk-in business." Indigo shrugged and offered baby Elise a small cube of sandwich.

"The food's ready to eat as soon as someone says the blessing." Maria slid another platter of sandwiches onto the counter and stepped back.

"I'll do it." Betsy smiled and reached for Jade's hand before bowing her head. "Heavenly Father, thank You for this food and the rain. Thank You most of all for the family You've blessed us with. Help us to honor You. Amen."

Murmurs of "Amen" came from the gathered crew.

Jade glanced down the long line at the counter but didn't see Tommy. Joaquin was there, though. Morgan and Skye were missing. Royal had explained that Sophie was working. Cyan hardly ever joined them for lunch, preferring to push through so he could finish work around the time Calvin got home from school. That might change when school got out in a couple of weeks. Would Olivia be here then, too?

"Here's some soup, hon. Nothing quite like grilled cheese and tomato soup on a rainy day." Betsy set a bowl down in front of Jade before offering the sandwich platter.

Jade took one of the golden-brown squares, the cheese leaking out the side and singeing her thumb. "Ooh. They're hot. Be careful."

"Have you heard from Olivia?" Betsy cut her grilled cheese in half diagonally before biting off a corner.

"I haven't. Tommy has. Nothing much more than a quick hi, though. I guess she has to be careful that Mel doesn't find the new phone." Was it wrong to have given the device to Olivia? There probably were other ways to have handled it—but most would have needed Mel's cooperation, and it was pretty clear that was never going to happen.

"Sorry. I know that's tricky." Betsy offered a sympathetic smile.

"Actually, I was thinking before I came down for lunch that, if things go like they're supposed to, Liv might be here for the summer. I know she won't have schoolwork to do, but she might still like to have a desk in her room, and I thought I'd move my office out to the living room, since she'll be here so much longer. I want her to have her own space, you know?"

Elise nodded. "It's nice to have a little space to call your own when you're that age. It was something the girls all complained about when we were living on the bus."

Jade shuddered. She couldn't imagine growing up on a converted school bus like her half-siblings had. They didn't seem to mind, but she still wasn't signing up any time soon.

"Is the living room going to be quiet enough for you to get your work done?" Betsy frowned.

Jade picked at her food. It was a good question, and she didn't know how to answer it.

"Why don't you move your office into my second bedroom?" Elise leaned forward so she could see around Betsy. "I'm hardly ever in the cabin—I'm usually over with Indigo either helping with the baby or with the orders."

"And the spinning and the dyeing. You've been a big help, Mom. You can practically run the shop on your own." Indigo flashed a grin at her mother.

"Are you sure I wouldn't be in the way?" That was a better solution. There was already a desk there, so she could set up her files and calendar and leave them. She'd only have to lug her laptop back and forth each day, and that wasn't exactly challenging.

"Completely sure. Why don't you go over after lunch and set up? I haven't touched the space since you moved out. The door's unlocked." Elise dunked the last bite of her grilled cheese into her soup before popping it into her mouth.

"Thanks, Elise. That's a perfect solution." Plus, it would give her more distance from Tommy. The way things were going, that wasn't a bad thing. She sighed.

"Are you okay?" The concern in Betsy's eyes had Jade's eyes filling.

She blinked back the tears and nodded. "I'm fine."

Her grandmother gave her a long look. "You know you can talk to me any time, right?"

"I do. Thanks, Grandma."

Grandma's smile flashed and she reached over and patted Jade's arm.

Jade's phone buzzed in her pocket. She slipped it out, her eyebrows lifting. "Will you excuse me? This is Olivia."

"Of course, hon."

Jade slid off her stool and strode down the hallway. She peeked in the first open door and found an empty bedroom. She tapped to accept the call as she shut the door behind her. "Hi, Livy."

"Jade?" The girl sniffled.

Jade's heart started to pound. "What's wrong? Are you okay?"

"Everything's wrong." It was hard to make out the words between the sobs.

"Tell me."

"You can't tell Dad."

Jade winced and lowered herself into the rocking chair that was in the corner of the room. "Livy, if you need help, your dad needs to know. I can't do anything on my own."

"You could call Don, couldn't you? I want to come live with you. Permanently."

"What's going on? You know we'd love to have you here. You know that, right?"

In the middle of the sniffle was a muted agreement.

"But we need the details to push." Didn't they? This was all Tommy's side of things. How much could she do before he got angry that she was interfering? Or maybe he wouldn't? She just didn't know anymore.

Olivia took a shuddering breath. "Some of the girls in my class took a video of me changing for gym class. They shared it with some of the guys and they put it online and now everyone's seen it. And I hate going to school. They all laugh at me."

And they were probably calling her names, too. Jade's heart broke. "Oh, honey. What did your mom do?"

"She said these things happened and maybe this would motivate me to lose the fifteen pounds she wants me to lose."

"Oh, Olivia." Jade had never considered herself a violent woman, but if Mel had been accessible, she would have been put to the test. "There's so much wrong with that. Has the school done anything?"

"They tried to suspend me."

"Because?"

Olivia's voice was a mumble. "I made a meme making fun of them and put it online."

Jade closed her eyes.

"I know it was wrong, but no one was doing anything about the video."

"I understand. So when you were getting suspended, the school finally found out about what they did?"

"Yeah."

"And?"

"And we all have a warning in our file and there won't be any leniency next time."

That was good. So many schools had a zero-tolerance policy that swept the victims up along with their abusers. It was too bad the others hadn't had a just punishment, though. "When is school out?"

"Two weeks." The dread in her voice said everything Jade needed to know.

"I'll call Don and see what we can do. I love you, Olivia. So does your dad. Hang in there, okay?"

"Okay. I gotta go, I hear Mom."

The call disconnected. Jade cradled her head in her hands. Calling Don was the right thing. Should she tell Tommy first? Let him call Don?

Olivia had asked her not to. Was Jade even supposed to share details with the lawyer? Oh, this was a mess.

Still, Olivia came first. To Jade and to Tommy. Maybe that would be enough to make everything work out.

Jade opened a browser on her phone and searched for attorneys in Albuquerque named Don. Thankfully, he had his photo on his website. Jade navigated to the "contact us" page, found the number and tapped the phone icon beside it.

20

Tommy swiped mud off his face and squinted up at the sky. At least for now the rain was holding off and there were just heavy, black clouds overhead. They'd gotten the posts in, thankfully, before the rain. So now it was a matter of cross beams—or at least that was the main task for today.

He probably could have gone back to the Hewitt's house for lunch. Or to his cabin to see Jade. But Skye's invitation to join her and Morgan for lunch had seemed easier. Especially since he had a sandwich with him.

He wasn't avoiding Jade.

Or, not exactly.

Tommy sighed and took a few steps back. "It's looking good."

"It sure is. This thing will be a lot of fun for the youth groups. Not sure about the missionary trainees—or whatever they are—but high school kids are going to think it's the best." Joaquin climbed down from the top of a set of higher than usual monkey bars. "Time to call it?"

"Yeah, probably. But we got a lot done today, despite the rain."

"Definitely. Should finish up early next week?"

"That's my guess."

Joaquin nodded. "You driving back to the cabins?"

Tommy couldn't think of a reason not to. "Need a lift?"

"If you don't mind. I walked back after lunch so I could spend a little extra time with Indigo and baby Elise."

Tommy laughed. "Is she going to be baby Elise forever?"

"Probably?" He shrugged. "We knew it might be an issue, but it'll be fine."

It was probably no different than calling someone Junior. Or Trip. But it wouldn't have been Tommy's preference.

"Sorry about the mud." Joaquin climbed into the passenger side of the truck.

Tommy winced. There was no escaping it. It wasn't like he was clean, either. He shrugged. "It's a truck. I'll be fine."

"Next sunny day, I can help you vacuum it out if you want."

"Nah." Tommy climbed in and cranked the engine. He fought another sigh before turning the truck toward home. Why was he so hesitant? He should be thrilled to get home after a dirty, sweaty, rainy, day. There was a hot shower. Clean clothes. And a good-looking woman.

"You all right, man?"

"Yeah. Course. Tired, I guess." Tommy reached for the radio. He didn't feel like dragging out his phone and getting it wet and muddy. He'd left it in the glove compartment and it'd be fine there until he was clean and dry.

"Did you hear from Jade?"

He shook his head.

"K. I was just wondering if you'd gotten any details about Olivia's call."

"Olivia called?" Tommy frowned. Maybe he should pull over and get his phone. Had he missed a call from his daughter? He glanced at Joaquin's hands, but they were just as dirty as his own.

"During lunch. I didn't catch much. She excused herself and went to one of the bedrooms. Probably just girl talk."

"Probably." A twinge of jealousy struck him right in the heart. Olivia was *his* daughter. She should have called him. But maybe she did. He hadn't kept his phone on him all day—there'd been no point with the rain and the mud. Impatience bubbled under his skin. He'd track Jade down and get the details. She could talk to him while he was in the shower.

They reached the cabins, and Tommy parked. "See you tomorrow."

"Yeah. If you want to shoot some aliens later let me know. Indigo's working on a sweater pattern, so she'll be muttering to herself and knitting all evening. I should have some time."

"Sounds good. I'll text you in a bit." Tommy glanced at the glove compartment, itching to get his phone. It could wait until he was dry. Ten minutes wasn't going to make a difference either way.

"Jade?" Tommy left his boots by the door and peeled off his wet socks before striding toward the bedroom. He stopped to poke his head in the second bedroom where Jade had set up her office. "Hey, hon, I'm . . . and you're not here."

He frowned. The desk looked different. Cleaner. And her laptop was gone. His stomach clenched.

"Jade?" He called a little louder this time and headed into their bedroom. Empty. The cabin wasn't big—he would have seen her if she was in the common areas, but he poked his head out to check she wasn't sleeping on the sofa.

Where was she? Did it have anything to do with Olivia's call? Not quite frantic, he turned the shower on to heat and shed his clothes quickly, dumping them into the hamper before stepping under the just-this-side-of-lukewarm spray. He lathered and rinsed while the water heated—adjusting it cooler after it finally got hot. Clean, he shut off the tap and roughed a towel over his hair before wrapping it around his waist.

He stepped out onto the bathroom mat. "Jade?"

Still no answer.

Tommy threw on clothes and jogged out to the truck to retrieve his phone. Six missed calls.

Six.

He opened the call log. There was one from Olivia around lunchtime—so she'd tried to call him. Some of the tightness around his heart eased. Except the other five were from Don. He hit the phone icon to return the call.

"This is Donald."

"Hi, Don, it's Tommy. I saw you called."

"Did you listen to my voicemail?"

Tommy pulled the phone away from his ear as he took the steps back into the cabin. Sure enough, the little voicemail light was on. "No. Sorry. You want me to do that?"

"I can give you the gist. Basically, yes, Olivia's wishes do matter at this point. I found a judge in the Colorado family court who's willing to hear a petition for a change in primary custody on Monday. It'd be better if you were there, but I can go up alone if you can't get away."

Tommy's mind started to spin. What brought this on? Sure, she'd said it when he was there, but he hadn't made the time to talk to Don about it. "I can come. We'd leave Sunday?"

"Yeah." There was a pause. "You sound confused, Tommy."

"A little."

Don sighed. "Talk to Jade."

"Jade?" What did Jade have to do with any of this? "Why Jade?"

"Because she's the one who called me and gave me the information to get this ball rolling."

"Information. What information?"

"Talk to Jade."

"I don't want to talk to Jade. I'm talking to you." Tommy frowned. "Don't give me any confidentiality stuff, either, Don. This is my daughter."

"I realize that. But the reality is that what I know was told in confidence and I was explicitly asked not to share details." Don cleared his throat. "Is it a problem to talk to Jade?"

"I just have to find her." Tommy scowled at the empty cabin. "Let me know if you want to go up together or just meet in Colorado."

"Okay. This is good news, Tommy. Focus on that."

Oh, sure. Tommy stared at the dark screen of his phone. Good news. Maybe it was—sort of. It wasn't a guarantee that Olivia would be able to come. And it wasn't right that all this was happening with him completely in the dark. Without him having been at the helm.

Guilt swamped him. Olivia had said she wanted to come live with him. He'd said he'd talk to Don. And he'd put it off—school would be over in a matter of weeks and it hadn't seemed urgent. Better to adjust over the summer.

The door creaked and he spun, his temper flashing. "Where have you been?"

Jade took a step back and eyed him warily. "At Elise's cabin. We talked at lunch about Olivia being here for the summer and making space for her and my office in a way that didn't impact our family space."

He scowled. It didn't matter that it was reasonable. Nothing was reasonable right now. "So you just move out?"

"I didn't move out. I moved my office." Her step fully into the house was tentative and she closed the door, but didn't push to latch it.

Tommy balled his fists but kept them tight against his leg. She looked scared. It was infuriating. It was heartbreaking. It shamed him. But he couldn't stop the words that boiled out of his mouth. "Why did I have to hear that I'm asking for primary custody from Don?"

Her face flushed red. "I was hoping to talk to you before he called."

"Were you? Seems to me you knew where to find me all day."

"You know what, Tommy? You're right. I did." Gone was the tentative, wounded animal. In its place was a furious woman. "And this is exactly why I didn't come find you. Olivia said she asked about coming here when you went up before Mother's Day. Don said today was the first he heard about it. She's being bullied. Her life is miserable. Mel isn't doing anything. It's our job as her parents to help her."

"You're not her parent! I am!" He hadn't meant to yell, but he stood there and watched his words hit her like a slap.

"You're right. I'm not. Maybe that's for the best all around." She strode past him, visibly leaving a huge gap that precluded any sort of physical contact.

"Where are you going?" He followed her into their bedroom, his heart clutching as he watched her dig out a duffel bag and start filling it with her things.

"I think maybe you had the right idea."

He frowned.

She glanced up and lifted her eyebrows. "You accused me of moving out. I think it's best I do."

"Jade." There was no air in his lungs. It strangled all the words in his head until he couldn't grasp their withered forms and speak them.

"Is it all right if I talk to Don about an annulment? Or maybe I'm better off with my own attorney. It might not be possible. But don't worry, if we have to divorce, I don't want anything more than what I brought into the marriage. I was never in this to take something from you."

Her words pierced his heart like arrows in a bullseye. "Jade. Don't do this."

She shook her head and brushed past him, leaving half of his body on fire. "I think I have to."

"Jade." He stood helpless and watched her stride through the cabin and out the door. She didn't slam it. In so many ways that would have been better. The quiet click held more finality.

Tommy slid down the wall and dropped his forehead on his knees.

Now what?

~

TOMMY GLANCED over at the passenger seat again, still not completely able to believe Olivia was sitting beside him as they drove back toward Hope Ranch.

"What?" Livy frowned at him. "Did I get something on my face?"

"No." He smiled and reached over to pat her leg. "I'm just happy."

"Me, too. Mom's pissed."

"Liv."

She hunched her shoulders. "Sorry. Angry. Is that better?"

"Much." The fact was, it didn't matter which word they used, Mel had surpassed any of the definitions. He sighed. The fight wasn't over. Don had already said as much. But Olivia stating clearly for the judge that she wanted to try living with her dad had been a big push in their favor. And having primary physical custody in New Mexico made it more likely that they could move the case to the local courts. That was all going to help Tommy keep Livy with him. It had to. "I wish you'd told me what was going on at school. I would have acted faster."

She jerked a shoulder and looked out the window. "It's embarrassing."

"You told Jade."

"Dad. She's a woman." She was so matter-of-fact that Tommy chuckled.

He remembered—barely—when life had been so cut and dry. "I'm still sorry."

"It's okay." She paused then turned back to look at him. "Why didn't Jade come? I really thought she'd be there."

Tommy focused on the road straight ahead. He hadn't talked to Jade since she left on Thursday. Now it was Tuesday. Oh, he'd tried reaching out, but she'd ignored him. Finally, Elise had let him know it was better if he gave her some space.

He was trying.

It was killing him.

"Dad?"

"Hmm?"

"Why didn't Jade come?"

He hated the suspicion in her voice. He cleared his throat. "She and I are probably over."

"What? You've only been married three months! You're not some Hollywood couple, Dad, you have to work this out."

He shook his head. It was tempting, so tempting, to tell her it was a grownup problem. But she'd quickly point out that she was thirteen and well on her way to adulthood. It wouldn't matter that there was a big space between thirteen and thirty.

"She loves you, Dad."

Tommy hadn't realized his heart could sink lower than the pit of his stomach. Surely there was a point when the weight that pressed down on him when he thought of Jade would break him completely. "I don't think that's true, hon. She loves you. You shouldn't ever question that. None of this is your fault."

"That's what you said when you and Mom broke up."

"It was true then. It's true now." He glanced over in time to see her swipe a tear off her cheek.

"I don't understand. She didn't let on that anything was wrong when I talked to her last week." Liv wiped her cheek again.

Tommy pinched the bridge of his nose. It didn't do anything to ease the tightness and pounding in his head. "I'm sorry, baby."

"You should tell Jade that." Olivia crossed her arms and shifted to stare out her window, effectively turning her back on him.

Hadn't he been trying? It was hard to apologize to someone who wouldn't look at you. Or speak to you. Or breathe the same air as you.

Hope Ranch often seemed like a small town to Tommy. Everyone was always right there, all up in everyone else's business. How had Jade managed to cut all of that off? No one treated him differently, but they'd formed an invisible wall around Jade that made it clear whose side they were on.

And they were right to be.

Betsy and Wayne had told him to pray. He had been. The content of those prayers probably wasn't what it needed to be, though. Mostly it was the word "please." Or "help." And then a ridiculous movie reel of the good times they'd had together for those three glorious months played on fast forward through his brain.

Tommy sighed. He should come clean. Olivia was already mad at him—was it better to rip all the bandages off at once? "I've tried to apologize, Livy, but there's more to the story than you know."

Olivia turned, scowling at him. "Like what?"

He licked his lips as the words stuck in his throat. "Well. Jade and I weren't actually a couple. Your mom was pushing me to sign away all my rights to you. I refused. She started arguing that you were better off with someone who was in a committed relationship, and I said I was."

"You lied."

"Yeah." Heat crawled up Tommy's neck. "I'm not proud of it. But then Don started talking about how it would make things easier, and I mentioned it in passing and before I knew it, Jade said she didn't mind pretending to be my girlfriend if it would mean you'd get to visit."

Olivia said nothing, but her eyebrows lifted up until they were nearly hidden by her bangs.

Tommy let silence settle in the cab of the truck. The rhythmic hum of the tires on asphalt was soothing.

"I don't understand."

"What don't you understand, Liv?"

"Why would you get married? Why wouldn't you just say no, it wasn't time yet, and put me off? Mom's always saying not now or wait." Olivia's eyes filled.

Where was he supposed to go from here? It had been more Jade's idea than his. But he hadn't protested loudly. He shouldered as much of the burden as Jade—more, since the benefit was his. And until last week, he'd been grateful, because Jade was everything he wanted in a wife. She was fun to be around and talk to, and they had chemistry. He was crazy about her. And she wanted nothing to do with him. "Do you want me to take you back to your mom?"

"No!" Olivia paled. "No. That doesn't have anything to do with this. I still want to live with you. Can I still see Jade sometimes?"

"Of course, honey. She's at the ranch."

"But she's not living with you?"

"Not right now."

"Do you wish she was?"

"More than you can imagine."

"Then you should fix it, Dad. Maybe I don't like how you guys went about this, but I love Jade. And I think you do, too?"

He gave a slight nod. It was hard to admit, even to himself. He'd messed this up so badly.

"So we'll fix it."

"She's pretty steamed. Rightfully so. It might be too late."

Olivia shook her head. "I don't believe that. I'll help, okay? Just trust me."

It was worth a try. Anything was worth a try. "I do. I'm glad you're coming home with me."

"I'm glad I don't have to see Mom and Steven again until fall break." Olivia managed a slight smile. "Don's pretty fierce in court."

Tommy chuckled. That was true. If only fixing things with Jade could be as easy. *Please, God. Help me fix this.*

"It's gonna be okay, Dad."

21

"There's someone to see you." Elise smiled gently before disappearing back into the hallway.

Jade sighed and saved her document. It wasn't as if she was making any progress this morning. She'd been staring at the back cover copy, letting the words run together rather than attempting to tighten them up for the author. It wasn't her favorite task, but she didn't dread it like it seemed some authors did. She was happy enough to be paid to do it for them.

She grabbed her coffee cup before padding out into the living room. Her heart swelled when she saw Olivia and she grinned. "There you are!"

"Oh, Jade." Olivia raced across the room and threw her arms around Jade, burying her face in Jade's shoulder. "This is a mess."

"You're telling me." Jade kissed the top of Olivia's head and shot Elise a pleading look. She didn't want to be alone without a buffer—or a witness—just in case.

Elise shook her head and started toward the door. She paused to wave goodbye before vacating the cabin.

Guess she was on her own. That wasn't bad. Not precisely.

She wasn't sure where she stood with Olivia, though. She gave the girl a squeeze and eased back. "I take it the judge ruled in your dad's favor?"

Olivia nodded. "In your favor, too. Right?"

"Of course. I'm glad you're here with Tommy full time. I hope that the school will treat you better. If nothing else, it's a new batch of kids, so you don't have the stigma from what happened. And you have the whole summer to shake it off." She paused. Was shaking it off the right way to phrase it? It wasn't a bad grade. Maybe Olivia needed to talk to someone with more professional credentials attached to their name. Would Tommy think of that? "If you want to talk to someone—a professional—make sure you let your dad know. So you can process everything and heal."

Olivia rolled her eyes. "Jade. I'm fine. I've been seeing a shrink since I was five."

"So you've already talked to someone?"

She nodded.

"Did you tell your dad you'd like to find someone here to keep up the therapy?"

She jerked her shoulder. "I don't think I need it."

Jade bit her lip. "I hope that's true. Keep it in mind, okay? Especially since . . . why don't we go sit down?"

Jade moved to the couch and perched on a cushion. She waited until Olivia sat next to her, then reached over and took her hand.

"What's going on?"

"Tommy and I aren't going to stay married. My lawyer is looking into an annulment—it's possible—but we'll get a simple divorce if that doesn't work out."

"Divorce is never simple." Olivia looked crestfallen.

Jade's heart bled. "I know that. This isn't easy for me."

"Then don't do it."

"I don't really see another choice. Your father made it pretty clear that I'm not an equal partner—" Jade cut herself off. This was too much information for a kid. Even a teenager. It wasn't right to burden Olivia with the problems of her hasty marriage to Tommy. "It doesn't matter. The point is that no matter how much I love you, it's best if I step away. But we can still be friends. I hope we'll still be friends."

Olivia snorted. "Now you sound like you're breaking up with me."

Jade's lips twitched. "I guess it does. That's the opposite of what I want to do."

"Don't you want to be married to Dad?"

"What I want isn't the issue here."

"Isn't it?"

She sighed. "This is going to come out like the kind of adult I never wanted to be, and I'm sorry, but this just isn't something you're going to understand. It's complicated and I don't want to burden you with it."

"You mean the stuff about how you and Dad were only pretending to be a couple to give Dad a leg up with custody and then got married because I was pushy about it?" Olivia looked smug.

Jade kept her jaw from dropping. Barely. He'd told her? Tommy had laid it all out like that? Jade looked away. "You must think I'm crazy."

"Nah. Dad's hot. For an old guy."

"It's more than that." Jade turned her gaze on Olivia and shook her head. "But none of it matters. At the minimum it's for him and me to figure out."

"Don't you have to talk to him for that to happen?"

"Olivia. That's enough. I'm happy to spend time with you. I would *like* to spend time with you. I'm really glad you're here at Hope Ranch and that it's working out for your dad to have you full time. You need to let the rest of it go though, okay? It's not your business."

A sulky pout started to form. "I'm not a baby."

"No, you're not. You're a lovely young woman." Jade held up her hand when Olivia's mouth opened. "But there are still some things that are for adults to handle because they're more complicated and intricate than you're going to understand."

"Fine." Olivia frowned. "I don't want you to leave Dad."

"I love you, Livy. That's not going to change."

"That doesn't help."

How many times could one person's heart break? "I know, but it's the best I can do. I'm sorry."

JADE BROUGHT Betsy a cup of coffee and sat across from her in Elise's living room. It wasn't usual for her grandmother to stop by mid-morning, but it wasn't *un*usual either. To stay for coffee? That was less frequent.

Betsy sipped her coffee and smiled. "How are you doing? I feel like we never see you anymore."

"I'm okay. It just feels easier to avoid being around Tommy when I can." She wasn't always able to. The last two weeks with Olivia around had slipped into a bit of a routine. Liv would come and hang out most afternoons—so Jade had adjusted her work hours and let clients know she'd be more focused in mornings and later afternoon or evening times. So far, no one had minded. Liv was not-so-subtly continuing to push Jade and Tommy together. And Jade's heart was nowhere near mending.

"Have you talked to him? He looks as brokenhearted as you do." Betsy leaned forward and set her coffee aside. "It's not good for married couples to spend this kind of time apart without speaking. Living separately like the two of you are. It's not how you make a marriage work."

Jade's sigh was full of the exasperation she felt. "Our marriage isn't going to work! He doesn't want it to. He wanted help getting custody of Olivia, not someone to help him with her. I didn't realize there were lines I wasn't supposed to cross. Maybe I should have."

Betsy's eyebrows lifted. "Tell me what happened. I haven't actually heard the details."

Jade ran through the details quickly. She was tired of rehearsing things—not that she was able to keep from doing it at two in the morning—and not seeing anything she'd change. "So Don got a hold of him before I could and Tommy made it clear that Olivia was *his* daughter and I was not to ever act on her behalf."

"Ouch. If it matters, I think you did the right thing to keep Olivia's confidence."

"Thank you."

"However." Betsy smiled, her tone gentling. "Did you ask Olivia to tell her dad?"

"Yes. I pushed as hard as I felt comfortable pushing."

"Did you ask if you could tell Tommy for her?"

Jade blinked. No. That wasn't a solution she'd considered. And it might have worked. Her stomach sank. Could she have avoided this mess? "She might have said no."

"That's true. But if she was just too embarrassed to share the details with him, she might have been willing for you to serve as a proxy."

"Maybe. Except the way Tommy reacted to me reaching out to Don, I imagine Tommy would still have been angry that Olivia was comfortable telling me something but not him."

"Sure. And he needs to work on that if he's going to have a wife. Any wife. Because when two people get married, they form a family and no kids are off limits to the other. It doesn't matter whose blood they share." Betsy reached for her coffee. "Do you love him?"

"It doesn't matter. Even if I do, he doesn't love me. He doesn't respect me. Love isn't enough without friendship and respect."

"That's true. You don't think you have those?"

"I did. Until this whole situation with Olivia happened. He flat out said I wasn't part of any solutions that had to do with his daughter." Just thinking about it made her blood boil again. At least the anger masked the ache. Because his words had cut deeper than she would ever admit out loud. "Now? No. I'm sure we don't."

"Oh, honey. I think you're wrong." Betsy sighed. "Why won't you talk to him?"

"What's there to say?" She didn't want to have a big fight and dig through all the reasons why she wasn't good enough to be a real part of his family. She'd offered to help and that usefulness had come to an end. It was better to admit defeat and move on before it got even more complicated.

"You could try telling him how you really feel."

"Surely he can figure that out? Even someone as emotionally ignorant as Tommy has to know when he's tromped all over someone's heart and set it on fire." She wasn't going to go begging him to love her. Being too willing to accept whatever small bit he was offering had gotten her here in the first place. "Sometimes, I think you have to cut your losses."

"So stubborn." Betsy probably hadn't intended Jade to hear the muttered words. "You're a lot like your father. He was never able to let go of an injury—imagined or real."

Imagined? Did Betsy think Jade had concocted this whole situation? She crossed her arms. "Sometimes self-preservation has to take a front seat."

Betsy's smile was sad. "So Martin liked to say. Oh, not in so many words, but the meaning is the same. Jade, honey, please don't harden your heart. I know it feels safer. I do. But it isn't what Jesus asks of us."

Jade blinked.

"At least try to talk to Tommy and clear the air? If you're determined to divorce him, no one is going to be able to stop you. But don't do it full of hurt and bitterness. At least try to hear him out and forgive him."

Ugh. It was probably the right thing to do, but she didn't want to. So many things—from sermons to songs and now her grandmother—had all said the same. "I guess I can try. But I don't think it's going to change anything."

"Will you keep an open mind?"

"I guess."

Betsy nodded. "Thank you. I've been praying. I plan to continue."

Jade closed her eyes. Praying. She'd done some of that. Then she'd stopped. "Can I ask you a question about that?"

"Of course. Always."

"Do you think it's possible this all happened because God was mad that we got married to make Tommy's custody case stronger? I mean, marriage is a big deal to God, right? So maybe He's sort of swatting us back?" And if that was the case, what was He going to do if she went through the divorce? It was one of the reasons she hadn't given her lawyer instructions one way or the other. Jade really didn't need God chasing her around because He was angry.

"No. That's not how God works." Betsy frowned. "Do you think He's sitting in heaven watching people and waiting to dump bad things on them if they sin and good things if they don't? He's not a vending machine, where you get out what you put in."

Of course He wasn't. "I didn't mean—or not consciously. I guess there's still enough of my mom in me that I worried."

"It's natural enough. People act that way plenty. But not God." Betsy paused a moment, but she seemed to be thinking—collecting her thoughts—so Jade waited. "We all make choices. Every day, right? Hopefully, we're walking closely with the Lord and so our choices reflect His desires for us because we're so closely following His Word. But sometimes we go off our own way. And He'll let us. But then we end up with consequences that we might not have chosen. And even though He'll forgive us when we ask, that doesn't always negate the consequence. Look at Joaquin and Indigo."

Jade managed a small smile. Her half-sister Indigo and her now-husband Joaquin had definitely made a choice that resulted in a consequence. Baby Elise was an adorable consequence. And watching the people at the ranch love both Indigo and Joaquin without lectures and harangues was one of the major reasons Jade had been willing to listen when they talked about Jesus. "I guess that makes sense. Do you think we made a mistake?"

"I don't think that matters now. The fact is, you and Tommy are married. God hates divorce. Which doesn't mean everyone has to stay—if there's adultery or abuse, for example, God doesn't ask you to stay and put yourself in danger. I do believe sometimes, with repentance, a marriage that's suffered infidelity can be healed. But that's up to the people involved and the—hopefully Godly—counsel they receive."

If those were the only reasons divorce was okay, Jade wasn't in a great spot. There was no clause for "Oops, I jumped too fast and didn't think it through."

"So you think we need to try to work it out."

"I do."

Jade's eyes burned. It was what she wanted. She missed him

—most of the time she was able to squash those feelings, but they were still there. And yet. "He'd have to be willing to change his stance on Olivia. She'd be—well, right now she already is—my stepdaughter. I'd want to be able to act on her behalf without having to run everything past him."

"I can understand that. I'll go back to your needing to talk to him. Tell him, not me. Listen when he talks."

Instead of flying off the handle and running off. Right. Jade scrubbed her hands over her face. "Okay. I'll give it a shot. Thanks, Grandma."

"It's my pleasure. I love you, Jade. I think maybe you've gone too long without hearing those words. You're not alone anymore."

A hot lump lodged in her throat. She stood and crossed to the couch so she could sit beside her grandmother and rest her head on her shoulder. Betsy slipped her arm around Jade and squeezed her close.

She'd married Tommy in part to solidify her place in the family—like it was something she had to earn. Maybe that wasn't true. Maybe she'd had a place all along.

22

Tommy stared into his coffee. He didn't have the energy to lift it and sip. What was the point, anyway? Before too much longer, he was going to be a twice-divorced loser. Would Mel take that and run to the judge to try and get Olivia back? Don continued to say that wasn't going to be possible, but how was Tommy supposed to relax?

Olivia was settling in. Thriving.

And Jade. He missed her. She was right next door, but she might as well be on the other side of the country. Or the world.

He'd had enough time to think in the four weeks of sleepless nights since he'd shot off his mouth. And he'd been wrong. He knew it. He'd known it as he was driving to Colorado. Honestly, he'd known it pretty much the minute Jade shut the door behind herself.

"Dad?"

He looked up and forced a smile. "Morning, baby. How'd you sleep?"

Olivia shrugged. "Can I have some coffee?"

"Yeah." He'd lost that fight pretty fast. Without Jade to back him up, he hadn't been able to stave off his daughter's arguments. She'd presented them logically. He had to give her that. And so far at least she'd only had one cup a day. How much damage could that really do to her system? She didn't drink soda or anything else that was bad.

Olivia rattled around in the kitchen. After a minute, she took a seat at the table with an untoasted frozen waffle and her mug of coffee.

"How can you eat them like that?"

"I don't know. I like them." She crunched into the waffle. "What are we doing today? It's Saturday. You don't have work, right?"

"No. No jobs today. What do you want to do?"

Olivia gave him a long look. "You don't want to do anything, do you?"

"I want to spend time with you."

"I know that, Dad. But since I live here now, maybe we don't have to spend that much time together." She paused and sipped her coffee. "Could I go horse riding?"

"Sure, we can do that." Horseback riding wasn't even on the list of things he wanted to do, but that was dad life sometimes. "I'll give Morgan a call."

"I have a better idea."

"What's that?"

"How about I go see if Sophie's free? She and I could go for a ride. Or maybe Calvin could come too. Then you can sit here and mope into your coffee alone."

He bristled. "I'm not moping."

"Okay."

Tommy frowned and finally lifted his mug to his lips. Her "okay" had been filled with entirely too much disbelief.

"Maybe . . ."

He looked at her when she didn't continue.

"I just think maybe if you had some time without work and

without me, then you could go next door and fix things with Jade."

Tommy closed his eyes. "Liv."

"Dad."

He sighed.

"When's the last time you tried? It's been at least a week." Olivia drained her coffee and pushed her chair back. "I'm going to change and see about that ride. Talk to Jade. Please, Dad? For me?"

Maybe if he said Olivia had sent him, Jade would actually give him a minute of her time. "I'll try."

Olivia threw her arms around his neck from behind and kissed his cheek. "Thanks. Don't worry about me. If the ride doesn't work out, I'll go hang with Betsy and Wayne. They're always good for a game of Chinese checkers."

He smiled and watched her disappear toward her bedroom. At least someone was headed toward a good day.

Tommy drained his coffee, stood and moved to the kitchen, where he set his mug in the sink. His stomach was already twisting unhappily. Maybe a shower would provide some much-needed clarity. He had to to apologize for pushing her away, but just how much groveling would it take to get in the door?

After spending too long under the pounding hot water—long enough that the water was starting to cool—Tommy dressed in jeans and a collared shirt and headed out of the cabin. His footsteps grew slower and heavier. He stopped at the bottom step of the cabin Jade now shared with Elise. He couldn't quite make himself take that next step.

He closed his eyes. This was a horrible idea. How many times was he supposed to get kicked in the teeth? Deserved? Sure. Yes. Absolutely. But how was he going to apologize and try to make it right if she refused to even be in the same room?

The cabin door opened and Elise smiled at him from the doorway. "You coming in?"

"No. I don't think—"

"Tommy. Come in." Elise lifted her eyebrows and stepped back.

He sighed, then trudged up the steps and through the door.

"Why don't you make yourself comfortable in the living room? Can I get you some coffee?" Elise hovered near the kitchen.

"No. Thanks." Tommy perched on the edge of the couch. "Would you be willing to let Jade know I'm here?"

"Oh, no." Elise smiled. "I'm on my way over to open the shop for Indigo. She's moving around though, so I don't imagine it'll be long. I'll be praying the two of you can figure this out."

"I—" Tommy broke off when Elise lifted a hand and slipped out of the cabin. He swallowed and clasped his hands in his lap. Well.

He dragged his phone out of his pocket and tapped on his web browser to scroll the news. Maybe there was something going on in the world that would keep his mind off the upcoming argument with Jade.

It was sure to be an argument.

She didn't seem like the kind of woman who was going to let him apologize and then have an end of it.

"What are you doing here?"

He looked up. His breath caught. She was so pretty—even mad. And there was no question that she was mad. "I was hoping to have a chance to talk to you. To apologize. Elise let me in when she was leaving."

Jade studied him a moment before nodding.

What did that mean? "I'm so sorry. I should never have said that about you not being Olivia's family. You are. Even if—"

"Even if?"

He shook his head. He wasn't going to open the door to a conversation of about ending things. "No qualifications. You're part of her family. And the fact is, your action made it possible for Liv to be here. I didn't act when I should have. So I owe you my gratitude as well as an apology. Is there any way you can forgive me?"

"You hurt me."

He closed his eyes. The pain in her voice drove home, again, how badly he'd messed up. "I know. I don't have anything more I can offer besides an apology. If I could go back and change it, I would. I've replayed the conversation in my mind more times than I care to count. There's no excuse."

Jade pressed her lips together. "Okay. Thank you."

"You'll forgive me?" He couldn't help the hopeful plea at the end of his words. Maybe it laid too much of his heart bare, but at this point, he was willing to be vulnerable if it would open the door to fixing things.

"I will. I do." She sighed and came to sit beside him on the couch. "I'm sorry, too. I should have come to the camp to talk to you. I still don't think I would have betrayed Olivia's confidence—"

"No. You did the right thing. Livy needs to know she can trust you. I was off base there. Jealous." That hurt to admit. But it was true. He'd spent so long fighting against alienation attempts by Mel that he'd leapt to conclusions and hurt without stopping to think.

"You get that it's easier to talk to someone who's the same gender as you about some things, don't you?"

"Now I do. I hadn't thought about it." Tommy shrugged. "It's still hard to swallow. She's my little girl. I don't want her to think she can't come to me about something. I don't like knowing there are things she'd rather not come to me about. I'll get over it. Or at least I'll try to understand it."

"I guess that's all anyone can ask. If it helps any, some of her reticence seems to have been that Mel blew it off. And she did it in such a harsh, dismissive way that Olivia wasn't sure if she was right to be upset."

"That only makes it worse." He hurt for his daughter and he was angry—again—at Mel. Would there ever come a time when his ex-wife's actions wouldn't send his blood pressure soaring? "Are we okay, Jade?"

"I guess it depends on what you mean by that."

Before he could check himself, Tommy reached for her hand. "I want us to go back to where we were. I don't want to lose you. I love you."

Jade looked away, but she didn't move her hand.

What was she thinking? Part of him wanted to keep talking—to plead his case. But silence was probably the better choice.

Jade sighed. "Are we friends, Tommy?"

Where did that come from? "I think so."

"Do you respect me?"

He swallowed. These questions couldn't be good. Had he botched things up so badly that there was no going back? "Yes. So much."

Now Jade did pull her hand away. She pressed her palms together in front of her face and bounced her fingers against her lips. "I don't want a divorce. But I also don't want a marriage where I have to run everything by you before I act. There has to be trust. Respect."

"I understand that."

She sent him a withering look.

He stiffened. "I do. I realize I messed up. I've owned that. I haven't made excuses—or tried to justify my behavior. And I could. I could make a case that would explain why I responded the way I did. It wouldn't make it right, but it might help you see it wasn't that I don't trust and respect you. Do you need that? Is an apology not enough?"

"I'm not the bad guy here, Tommy."

"And I am?"

She closed her eyes. "No. I don't know. You hurt me. I forgive you. I'm not sure about going back to where we were though. Maybe a little bit of caution is better late than never."

His stomach plummeted and his mouth went dry. "Okay. What does that mean?"

"Betsy said something yesterday that got me thinking. We haven't really been putting God first in our relationship."

Wayne and Betsy had been busy. Wayne had cornered him and made a similar comment. Tommy's initial response had been to argue—he'd been praying about the idea since they first agreed to the fake relationship. But he'd finally come around to the fact that he'd made a decision and then asked God to bless it. He hadn't asked what God wanted them to do. "No. That's true."

"We need to do that."

That sounded great. "How? What does that mean to you?"

"You're supposed to be the family's spiritual leader, aren't you?"

He laughed. "Sure. Does that mean I can't ask for help?"

"I guess not. Maybe we should start with something simple like praying together—you and me and maybe also with Olivia."

That was a good idea. He nodded. He wanted Liv to see that Jesus was someone worth having in her life. Sure, going to church and being around people who prayed at meals was a start, but there was more to life as a believer than that. "That sounds like a good place to start."

Jade didn't respond.

He cleared his throat. "You know that means you'll have to be willing to spend time with me. With us."

Jade's smile was sad. "That's not a problem. I haven't enjoyed avoiding you. This hasn't been easy for me, either."

"That's good to know."

She frowned. "Why wouldn't you know that already?"

"You made it look pretty simple to walk away and not look back. I know I hurt you. You hurt me, too." She still was, for that matter. He'd said he loved her. She hadn't acknowledged it. Hadn't reciprocated it. How much of his heart was he supposed to lay out in front of her? Wayne said all of it. He'd said that marriages didn't survive when people were guarding their hearts. Everyone in the marriage had to be all-in, or no one was going to win. "Mel made it clear I was easy to leave. You backed her up."

"Oh, Tommy. No." She took his hand and clasped it to her heart. "It's been killing me."

He leaned closer, until their lips were just a breath apart.

Jade shifted away. "I can't. Not yet."

"Right." He turned his head and stared at the empty kitchen.

"Tommy—"

He held up a hand. "It's fine. I get it. I have to prove myself first."

"It's not about proving yourself. It's back to putting God first in our marriage." She crossed her arms, looking for all the world like a woebegone child who needed a hug.

His arms itched to draw her close and provide that comfort. But if she was going to throw it in his face, he'd save himself the humiliation of another rejection. He stood. "I know Olivia would enjoy having you around more if you can fit it in your schedule."

"I'd like that, too." She was watching him warily.

"Then I guess I'll let you get back to your Saturday. Thanks for seeing me." His voice sounded stiff to his ears, but what else was he supposed to do? She didn't want to go back to where they'd been. She wasn't giving him very many clues about what she did want. They could pray together—he was happy to do that—but when? He'd just follow her lead.

"Wait. Are you angry?"

He forced himself to tuck his hands in his pockets rather than crossing his arms. There was no need to look as defensive as he felt. "No. Not angry."

She cocked her head to the side. "What then?"

"Hurt. Confused." He shrugged. "Pick one."

"I don't understand."

"Yeah. Neither do I." He blew out a breath. "I want to fix things with you, Jade, but I don't know how. We're married. I get that we need to do more praying together, and I'm fine with that. I welcome it. I just don't know how we do that if you're still living somewhere else."

"I . . ."

"See? Maybe take a look at your calendar and let me know when you can work me in. We can go from there."

"That's not fair, Tommy."

"Yeah, well, it's the best I can do. I'm sorry." He headed through the door and out into the sunshine. That hadn't gone well.

Not well at all.

God? I could use a lot more help here.

23

Jade watched Tommy close the door and sank onto the couch with a sigh. She prayed for wisdom for the thousandth time today and waited. There was no response. No grand solutions popped into her head. The whole time Tommy was here, it had been all she could do not to throw herself into his arms and declare her love. That wasn't the right move. She knew that much.

Tommy had said they were friends. She tended to agree. He said he respected and trusted her. Other than the issue with Olivia—and it was a big issue—she was willing to admit he did demonstrate that.

He said he loved her.

Her heart jumped at the thought. She loved him. She wanted this to work.

She owed him an apology, too.

Jade jumped up and rushed to the door. She yanked it open. She'd search the ranch and tell him. This was stupid. It was time to set aside her hurt—her injured pride—and actually forgive like she said she would.

She nearly ran into him. He was sitting on the front step with his head in his hands. "Tommy?"

His shoulders sagged.

Jade closed the door before sitting beside him on the steps, close enough that their legs pressed against each other. "I'm sorry."

He turned to look at her, confusion on his face.

"It's easier to be mad. That's always been my go-to. It's safer. Push people away first, then they can't reject you, you know?"

He nodded.

"You said you love me." She paused, swallowing the first edge of nervousness that was trying to crawl up her throat. "I love you, too."

"You do?"

She nodded. "I just—it's not enough on its own."

"But it's a good place to start. Along with friendship. Respect. Trust." His gaze didn't waver from hers.

Was he looking into her soul? She got lost so quickly in his eyes. "It is."

He leaned forward and rested his forehead on hers.

"Can I come home?"

He closed his eyes. "Yes."

"Thank you." Jade shifted and touched her lips to his. There was work to do still, but they didn't have to go back to ground zero.

Tommy leaned back and slipped his arm around her shoulders. "Maybe we can talk to Betsy and Wayne. Do you think they'd do couples counseling with us?"

"That's a lovely idea. And if they don't feel comfortable, we'll talk to the pastor. I want to make this work. I want to put in the effort." Jade rested her head on his shoulder. "You're worth it. I'm sorry I made you think I didn't see that."

He gave her a gentle squeeze. "We'll get this figured out."

Marriage was hard. Why had she thought it would be an easy thing to jump into a marriage just to help Tommy out? "I hope so. It's still important for you. And for Olivia."

"And for us."

His words warmed her. She nodded. "And for us."

"Olivia was going to try to rope Sophie and Calvin into a horseback ride. You want to see if we can catch up to them?"

Jade hadn't done a lot of riding since she'd come to Hope Ranch, but she'd gone a few times. It wasn't high on her list of things she loved, but she enjoyed spending time with Liv. And with Tommy. She glanced at the leggings and tunic she wore. "Let me run in and change and then sure. Let's give it a shot."

Jade hurried back inside and changed into jeans and the riding boots that Betsy had given her. She pulled her hair into a ponytail low on her neck. It made the helmet easier to wear. Ready, she headed back out to find Tommy on his phone.

"No, Don. I haven't talked to Mel since we were in court. Or heard from her. I don't know if Livy has." He smiled and lifted his eyebrows when he noticed Jade. He held up a finger and pointed to the phone. "She's out riding. Jade and I were going to go see if we could catch up. If we do, I'll ask if her mom has been in touch and let you know. Should I be worried?"

It seemed like the answer was yes, but that was her. Mel wasn't one to be out of contact. Especially now that Olivia was here at the ranch.

"Yeah, okay. Thanks, man." Tommy ended the call and frowned.

"What's up?"

"Mel's lawyers reached out to Don to see if he'd heard from her. I guess after we won the custody hearing, she said some stuff that got them worrying and they haven't been able to reach her." He shook his head and stood. "Let's go see if we can find Liv."

"She has her phone, right? Why not give her a call?" Jade took Tommy's hand. Lacing her fingers through his was warm and comfortable. And it felt like home. They were going to make this work. "I'm still up for the ride, but it would make Don's life easier if you got back to him faster, right?"

"It would. You're right." Tommy tapped on his phone and held it to his ear as they walked. "If she's riding, she won't be able to answer though."

That was true. But maybe they hadn't gotten that far yet. Or maybe they were taking a break.

"Hi, Liv. It's Dad. Give me a call if you get a chance—Don wants to know if you've heard from Mom since you got down here. Jade and I are going to try and catch up with you. Bye." He shrugged. "No answer."

"All right. Worth a shot."

They rounded the bend and entered the stable. Horses poked their heads out over the stalls, always curious and hoping for snacks.

"You here to ride, too?" Morgan looked over from where he was spreading hay in the bottom of a stall. "Soph just took Calvin and Liv out. They left maybe twenty minutes ago."

"Did you get an idea of where they were heading?" Jade rubbed the nose of the horse nearest her.

"No. It's a nice day and the kids were excited. I'm guessing they're doing one of the longer loops. Were you going to try and catch them?" Morgan shook his head. "I don't know if you can."

Tommy glanced at Jade. "What do you think?"

There were a lot of trails at the ranch. She didn't really want to ride around aimlessly. "I doubt they'll be more than a couple of hours. They didn't take food."

Morgan laughed. "That's true. I didn't see a picnic."

"Let's just wait." Jade lifted her eyebrows. "We could walk

down to the camp and you can show me the obstacle course. I've heard it's a sight to behold."

Tommy laughed. "Olivia's been trying to break it in for us, but it's tricky. Sure. We can do that."

"You want me to have Olivia call you when they get back?" Morgan leaned against the stall door beside him.

"Would you? I left her a voicemail, but she doesn't always check." Tommy reached for Jade's hand.

"Sure thing. It's nice to see the two of you together."

Jade's face heated. It wasn't as if she'd tried to keep quiet about things falling apart, so she should probably have expected a comment here or there. But Morgan? He was usually so laid back.

"Thanks." Tommy squeezed her fingers.

When they'd left the stable and were on the path that would lead them to the camp, he bumped her shoulder. "Sorry. Should I not have taken your hand back there?"

"It's okay. People are going to find out—and I guess we want them to, right? I'm just embarrassed by my behavior." It was mortifying now to look back and see all the traps she'd fallen right back into. She'd given her life to Christ. She was a new creation. And yet all the old habits and self-defense mechanisms were alive and well. It would be so much nicer if putting her faith in Jesus had meant she was instantaneously able to stop sinning. Hopefully the people at the ranch would be as quick to extend grace to her now as they had been before.

Tommy stopped and pulled her into his arms. "There's nothing to be embarrassed about. It was a tough situation and we both reacted badly. These things happen. Do you know I've heard Betsy and Wayne yell at each other?"

Jade snorted out a laugh. The tension between her shoulders eased. "I have a hard time imagining it. They seem so perfect.

But Betsy told me that they didn't always get along like peas in a pod. I guess maybe I didn't believe it."

Tommy's lips pressed against her forehead before he released her and they started walking again. "Now you know."

They walked through the meadow. The camp lodge grew larger as they approached.

"This was the first walk I ever took here." Jade breathed in deeply.

Tommy shook his head. "I didn't know that."

"I was struggling to keep up with a very annoyed Indigo whose plan, I think, was to shove me into the dirt at Skye's feet and then storm off." She smiled at the memory. They'd come a long way—all of them—since the day she'd shown up intending to see how much trouble she could cause.

Tommy laughed. "I can see that. Did she?"

"No. We ended up having a good conversation. And honestly, the fact that she looked and walked like she wanted to murder me—but didn't actually take any of the cheap shots she could have—helped me start to realize how much I needed to change." Jade sighed. "Skye has never been anything but kind—but Indigo was honest, and I needed that, too."

"It's hard to fix things no one points out."

"Oh, people had pointed it out before. I just hadn't cared."

"There's that. I'm glad you came. I'm glad you stayed. And I'm glad you're willing to work with me."

Jade stopped and looked into Tommy's eyes. "Right back atcha."

They spent a half hour looking at the obstacle course. Jade tried a few of the elements, but rope climbing had never been one of her strengths, and it was one of the major entry points to the course.

Finished, they started back toward the ranch, laughing.

It was easy. Relaxed. And felt a lot like they were meant to do this forever.

Maybe they were.

The sound of horses carried over to them as they approached Indigo's sheep pens. Jade slowed to a stop and turned, shielding her eyes from the sun as she scanned the edge of the forest.

"There they are." Tommy pointed.

Jade followed with her eyes, finally spotting the three horses and riders coming out from one of the longer mountain trails. "They wouldn't have been able to get all the way to the top in that time, would they?"

He shook his head.

"I hope they're all right."

"I imagine they'd be going faster if something was wrong. My guess? Sophie has students she needed to get back for."

That made sense. "You want to meet them at the stables?"

He shrugged. "Sure."

"Are you worried about Mel at all?"

"I don't know. I don't want anything bad to happen to her. Not anymore." A ghost of a smile played on his lips. "I wasn't in such a healthy spot when we first got divorced."

Jade squeezed his hand. It was probably a natural thing not to be full of grace and love toward an ex. At least not at first. It was good that he had gotten there. "I don't, either. It would be bad for Olivia, if nothing else. For good or for ill, Mel is Liv's mom. I'm praying they can always have a good relationship. Preferably one that's better than I had with my mom."

"It's a good prayer." Tommy slowed as they approached the stable.

"Back again?" Morgan was tossing a jacket and insulated bag into the cab of his truck. "They haven't returned yet."

"We saw them heading this way, figured we'd meet up with

them here." Jade glanced at the horse noses as they walked together into the stable. "Do you have an a-p-p-l-e?"

Morgan laughed as the horses got excited. "They can spell now, apparently. But yeah, I'll go get some slices out of the fridge."

Tommy settled on a hay bale and propped one ankle on his knee.

Morgan came back with a small plastic bag. "Here you go."

Jade took the apple slices from Morgan with a grin. "Thanks."

"Any idea about how far out they were?" Morgan craned his neck as he looked out the stable door. "Oh. Never mind, here they are."

Tommy stood and followed Morgan out into the big space in front of the stable where people could mount and dismount more easily. Jade let them go and offered one of the apple slices to the first horse, enjoying the sensation of it delicately eating from her hand.

Several minutes later, Olivia flew through the doors and flung her arms around Jade.

Jade laughed. "Hi."

"Dad said he apologized and you forgave him so you'll still be my stepmom?"

Jade looked down into the hopeful expression and her heart filled. "We have some work to do, but yes."

"I love you, Jade."

Jade hugged the girl tight. "I love you, too."

24

"I don't see why you want me to bring my wedding dress." Jade frowned at Tommy, hands on her hips.

Tommy hid a smile. In the month since they'd patched things up, they'd been moving more slowly. More deliberately. They'd met weekly with Wayne and Betsy together. He'd been meeting with Wayne once each week on his own, and the men at the ranch had decided to have a morning Bible study together another day. Jade and Betsy were also meeting and the ladies were discussing a study of their own. It was good to be on solid footing.

"Well?"

"You don't like surprises, do you?"

"No. I really don't. I also don't understand why I should drag this enormous dress anywhere when there's no way you're going to cajole me into it."

He sighed. "I arranged for us to get some photos taken. We have the phone camera snaps that Don took, but I thought something more formal would be nicer. The square is lovely in the summer and the photographer has ideas."

Jade's face broke into a broad grin and she crossed the room to embrace him. "Oh, you sweet man. For that, I will bring the dress. And wear it."

He chuckled and kissed her. He'd meant it to be a short, perfunctory kiss—but, well, it was Jade and chemistry was the one area of their marriage they hadn't needed to work on.

"Are you guys ready—oops." Olivia laughed.

Tommy stepped back and shifted to glance at his daughter. "I had to spill the beans to get her to bring the dress."

"Jade." Olivia huffed out a breath. "I should have just snuck in here to get it."

"No. It's good. I'd rather know. I need a couple extra minutes to do more than the minimal makeup I was planning for dinner at the Cantina. I want to look good in the photos." Jade cocked her head to the side as she looked at Olivia. "What if we got you some lip gloss and mascara?"

Olivia's eyes went wide and she turned to face Tommy. "Can I, Dad? Please?"

"For tonight. Sure. But no growing up faster than you have to." Tommy winked. "I'll go wait in the truck, so don't you two take too long."

"Five minutes. Ten tops." Jade grinned and reached for Olivia's hand.

Tommy checked the time on his phone as he crossed through the cabin and out to his truck. When he was seated behind the wheel, he tapped out a quick text to let Joaquin know they weren't leaving quite yet.

The photos were definitely on the schedule. But he had one more surprise up his sleeve. Would she be okay with it?

He took a deep breath to settle the butterflies that had started to flutter around in his belly.

His phone buzzed with a response. Everything was ready whenever they got there. Hopefully it wouldn't be more than the ten minutes Jade had said.

Finally, his two ladies stepped through the cabin door. He smiled. Jade carried the bag holding her wedding dress. Olivia's dress was already hanging in the back seat.

"Ready?" He took the dress from Jade as she pushed it through the door. Twisting, he managed to snag the hanger on a hook and stuff the bottom of the dress down into the wheel well.

"Yes. And I have supplies to touch things up if we need." She held up a small cosmetic bag before setting it on the floorboards and reaching for her seatbelt.

"Ready, Liv?" He glanced in the rearview mirror to see his daughter clicking her seatbelt into place. She looked grown up with the touches of makeup. It cracked his heart, just a little. In five years, she'd be spreading her wings to leave the nest. It was what she was meant to do—but it didn't make it easier to let go. "You look beautiful."

Olivia blushed. "Thanks, Dad. You're pretty snazzy in your suit."

He'd thought about renting a tux, but hadn't been able to figure out how to do it without spoiling the surprise. "Thanks. Everyone set?"

He started the truck and backed out onto the ranch road. He'd put a Christian rock band on his phone and had it streaming quietly while Liv and Jade chattered. He contributed when he could, but was content to listen, too.

"She said she was sending me a present. I guess we'll see what it is when it comes. But it's pretty cool to have something from Japan, don't you think?"

Jade nodded. "I do. I still think it's odd that she and Steven just took off without letting anyone know."

"Not really. Mom's always doing stuff like that. Maybe not for a month, but they'd be gone two or three days sometimes without being in touch. You get used to it."

Tommy shook his head. "Why didn't you say something, honey?"

"I don't know. She made it seem normal. But I'm glad I'm here. A month with Gran and Gramps in the summer? Nuh-uh. They'd make me play golf with them." Olivia made a gagging sound.

Tommy laughed. "Not a golf fan?"

"I've never played. It really isn't fun?" Jade pursed her lips. "I think I'd like to try it once."

"Ugh. You and Dad can go. I'll hang out with Sophie. Did she ask you about me helping with some of her lessons? She was going to."

"She did. I said if you wanted to do that it was fine with me. You've got a good seat—if nothing else you can lead by example." Tommy smiled and turned into the church parking lot.

"Why are we at church?" Jade frowned as she scanned the parking lot. "Why are there cars here?"

"It's Wednesday. I'm sure there are always people at the church." Tommy resisted the urge to clear his throat. It wasn't a lie. It was Wednesday and weekdays tended to have groups that met in the church building. "As to why we're here, I thought it'd be easier to change here than a public restroom somewhere. The pastor said it was fine."

"Oh. That's actually really nice. I hadn't thought about that, or I would have suggested we change at the ranch."

Tommy nodded as he parked. He'd been dreading her bringing that up. His hope had been she wouldn't want to sit in the dress for the twentyish minute drive into town. Otherwise, he would have had to make something up to get them here. "Got your dress, Liv?"

Olivia beamed at him, her eyes sparkling with their shared secret. "Yep."

"All right, let's go on in." He unhooked Jade's dress and

draped it over his arm before reaching for Jade's hand.

Olivia took Jade's other hand and practically skipped to the church.

Tommy held the door for them, then nodded toward the hall. "He suggested using one of the classrooms down there. That's what they have brides do."

"Okay." Jade pressed her lips to his and took her dress. "We won't be long. I'll meet you here?"

"Sure thing."

Olivia shot him a thumbs-up behind Jade's back before she hurried after Jade.

When the hall doors closed behind the girls, Tommy hurried to the main worship center doors and peeked in. Their family—meaning the people who lived and worked at Hope Ranch—milled around inside. He blinked a few times before opening the door.

As one, they all turned to look his way.

"They're changing. Probably be just a minute or two." Tommy wiped his damp palms on his thighs. "Thanks for coming."

"You know we wouldn't miss it," Wayne said.

It was the truth. None of them would have missed it if there was any other choice. Because they were family. Maybe not by blood—although there was a lot of blood relation in there too—but even better, everyone there was family by choice.

He let the door shut and paced the foyer. It would be a few minutes, he was sure. Getting into a wedding dress had to be more of an ordeal than putting on jeans. Still, when Olivia poked her head out, Tommy's only thought was *at last.*

"Ready?"

Olivia nodded. "She looks even better than the first time."

"You remember what to do?"

"Dad. Yes." She leaned up and kissed his cheek before scurrying off to the worship center doors. She stepped inside and the softest strains of music starting worked their way out into the lobby area.

"Oh my goodness." Jade pushed through the door, clutching a handful of skirt. "I don't know what I was thinking. This dress is—"

"Stunning." Tommy laid a hand on his heart and mimed a fast beat. "You take my breath away."

Jade's face lit up and she brushed at the skirt of her dress. "Maybe I'll dig it out for the big anniversaries."

"I'd like that."

"Where'd Olivia go?" Jade looked past him, a tiny furrow forming between her eyebrows.

"She wanted to check something in the worship center. Let's go that way and get her."

"All right. I don't want to do a ton of walking in these shoes. They're just not made for it."

Tommy chuckled and took her hand. "I'll try to keep it to a minimum."

Olivia was about halfway down the aisle when they reached the doors. Tommy risked a quick glance at Jade as he grabbed the handle. It didn't look as though she'd clued in yet. He pulled open the door and stepped back.

Jade walked through.

Tommy joined her.

Everyone in the seats stood and the music changed.

Laughing, Jade turned to face Tommy.

"Jade Russell? Will you be my wife?"

Her eyes filled. She turned and looked toward Olivia, waiting for them now at the front of the room.

The pastor smiled at them.

Jade turned back, her gaze locking with his. "For as long as we both shall live."

EPILOGUE

Elise Hewitt watched with tears in her eyes as the last of her children—well, technically Jade wasn't her child, but neither of them cared about the details—got married. It was nice to see young people willing to bind themselves to one another legally and in the eyes of God.

And wasn't it amusing that God had found her after all these years? That He'd used Martin's parents to reach out? She sighed quietly.

Betsy Hewitt glanced over, smiled, and reached for Elise's hand.

Martin had been wrong about so many things. And Elise had never questioned any of them. They'd had good years together, mostly. Even though he'd never been the kind of man to stay in one place or confine himself to a single woman, he'd been good to her and their children.

And Jade seemed to have forgiven them.

Elise wanted to believe that Martin would have welcomed Jade and come to love her, too, if he'd lived. She wanted to believe a lot of things about Martin. Sometimes the questions gave her nightmares.

But now wasn't the time for thinking about that.

"It's my pleasure to re-introduce to you, Mr. and Mrs. Tommy Russell."

Elise clapped along with everyone else then stood as Jade and Tommy made their way into the crowd waiting for them.

"You really didn't suspect?" Olivia was grinning from ear to ear and clinging to Jade's hand. "Not at all?"

"Not one bit." Jade turned to Tommy and smiled.

Elise glimpsed the love shining in Jade's eyes—and reflected in Tommy's—and her heart sank a little. It was silly to be sad. Not everyone had the kind of love that filled fairytales and romance novels. Until she'd come to Hope Ranch, Elise would have said that kind of love was only possible in fiction.

Now, she'd seen it in action.

It all started with roots in the love of Christ.

She pushed her smile back into place and reached out to hug Jade as she neared. "I'm so happy for you, honey. As much as I've loved having you live with me, it's better that you're back with your family. Where you belong."

"You're my family, too, Elise." Jade kissed her cheek. "Don't ever forget that."

Elise nodded and focused for a moment on pushing the hollow feeling in her chest away.

She had family who loved her. Children and grandchildren, in-laws—her own and those of her children. She had Jesus.

She should be happy. Content.

At fifty-mumble, she certainly shouldn't be moping around and dreaming of love.

Talk about fairytales.

~

A note from Elizabeth...

It doesn't have to be a fairytale though, and Dave Fitzgerald might just be a real-life Prince Charming. Read Hope at Last, the final installment of the Hope Ranch series, today to find out

ACKNOWLEDGMENTS

Every book I write leaves me filled with gratitude for so many people in my life. First, I'm so thankful that Jesus continues to put stories in my head and give me the words to put on paper when I sit down to write.

I'm grateful for every reader who buys or borrows my books! I'm grateful for every review, every mention on Facebook or in random conversation with your neighbor about what you're reading. I'd still write the stories without readers, but knowing you're there makes it all feel so much more worthwhile.

I'm thankful for my husband and boys who give me space and time to work on my "kissing books" even though two of the three of them think the idea of a kissing book is pretty gross.

I'm grateful for the writer friends I've made as part of this journey - particularly Valerie Comer who also stands in as my beta reader, Lynnette Bonner who is not only a friend but an amazing cover designer, and Lesley McDaniel for her fantastic editing - but there are so many other amazing writers who I count friends that if I listed them all here, we'd be here forever and I'd probably still end up missing someone.

And as I sit here writing this, having just this week finished the first draft of the last book in this series, I'm grateful for my sister and my mom who were the first to encourage me to do anything more than email them the stories that I wrote. I don't know that I would have believed there were others who would appreciate my stories if they hadn't believed it first.

WANT A FREE BOOK?

If you enjoyed this book and would like to read another of my books for free, you can get a free e-book simply by signing up for my newsletter on my website.

OTHER BOOKS BY ELIZABETH MADDREY

Hope Ranch Series

Hope for Christmas

Hope for Tomorrow

Hope for Love

Hope for Freedom

Hope for Family

Hope at Last

Peacock Hill Romance Series

A Heart Restored

A Heart Reclaimed

A Heart Realigned

A Heart Redirected

A Heart Rearranged

A Heart Reconsidered

Arcadia Valley Romance – Baxter Family Bakery Series

Loaves & Wishes

Muffins & Moonbeams

Cookies & Candlelight

Donuts & Daydreams

The 'Operation Romance' Series

Operation Mistletoe

Operation Valentine

Operation Fireworks

Operation Back-to-School

Prefer to read a box set? Find the whole series here.

The 'Taste of Romance' Series

A Splash of Substance

A Pinch of Promise

A Dash of Daring

A Handful of Hope

A Tidbit of Trust

Prefer to read a box set? Get the series in two parts! Box 1 and Box 2.

The 'Grant Us Grace' Series

Wisdom to Know

Courage to Change

Serenity to Accept

Joint Venture

Pathway to Peace

Prefer to read a box set? Grab the whole series here.

The 'Remnants' Series:

Faith Departed

Hope Deferred

Love Defined

Stand alone novellas

Kinsale Kisses: An Irish Romance

Luna Rosa (part of A Tuscan Legacy)

Non-Fiction

A Walk in the Valley: Christian encouragement for your journey through infertility

For the most recent listing of all my books, please visit my website.

ABOUT THE AUTHOR

Elizabeth Maddrey is a semi-reformed computer geek and homeschooling mother of two who lives in the suburbs of Washington D.C. When she isn't writing, Elizabeth is a voracious consumer of books. She loves to write about Christians who struggle through their lives, dealing with sin and receiving God's grace on their way to their own romantic happily ever after.

facebook.com/ElizabethMaddrey
instagram.com/ElizabethMaddrey
bookbub.com/authors/elizabeth-maddrey

www.ingramcontent.com/pod-product-compliance
Lightning Source LLC
LaVergne TN
LVHW091047080826
845145LV00002B/651

* 9 7 8 1 9 4 7 5 2 5 0 4 7 *